AF609895

# Death after Kyoto

CARLOS ALEMAN

Edited by Jean Aleman

Copyright © 2017 Carlos Aleman

All rights reserved.

ISBN: 978-1546669371

# DEDICATION

To Jean. Your many years of binge watching Law and Order marathons have, no doubt, subconsciously had their effect upon me. However, I can't help, despite the inspiration of the hit series, twist the subject of crime drama into something otherworldly and strange. Thank you for your patience and love and your willingness to overlook any lapses in good judgment and taste.

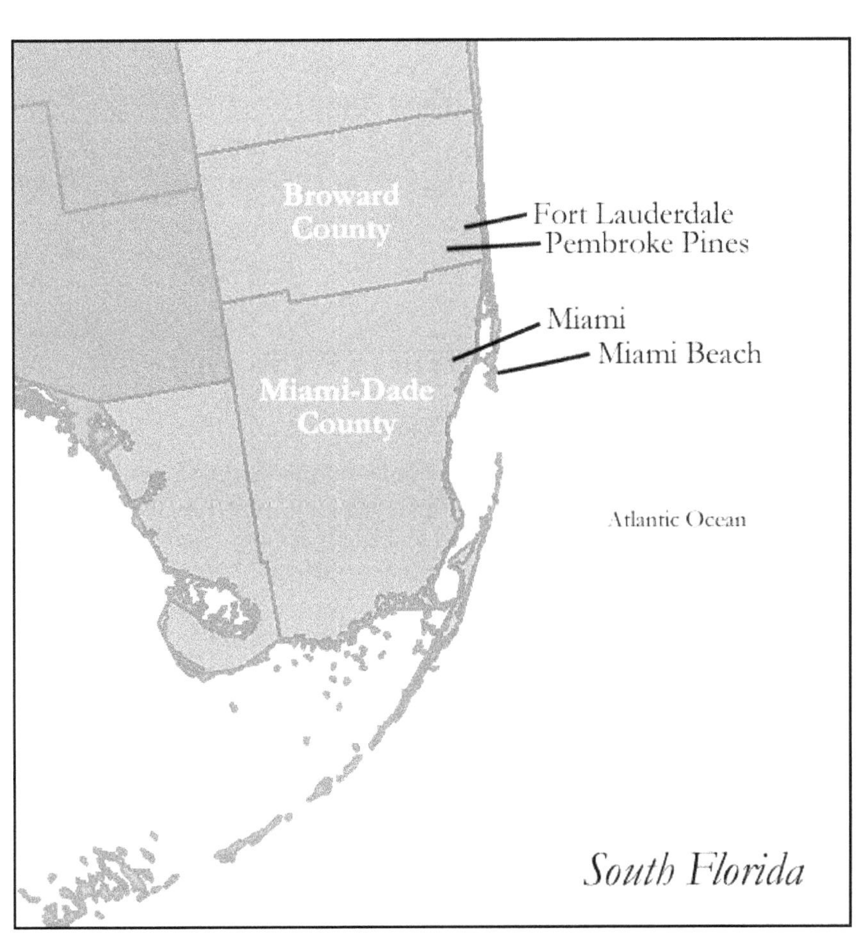
Broward County
Fort Lauderdale
Pembroke Pines
Miami
Miami Beach
Miami-Dade County
Atlantic Ocean
South Florida

# ABOUT THE COVER

The illustration is from a painting of a dragon I made when I returned from a trip to Asia in 2010. During the opening night of my solo art exhibit, a boy and his father were admiring it, so I later gave it to them. I hope it's worth a lot of money one day.

# CHAPTER ONE

The landing in Osaka had been a fascination to her for months. She had read about the Kansai airport online and watched a documentary about it on the National Geographic Channel. Knowing that the runway had been built on a technological marvel, one of the largest manmade islands in the world, exhilarated her and seemed to ward off the fatigue of the long trip that had begun in Florida.

Emily had been bearing a headache and thirst for many hours, making this the worst flight she had ever been on. Although the service had been excellent, she just hadn't been feeling well. But now that she had arrived at her destination, her body seemed to instinctively secrete whatever neurochemicals were necessary to help her function. She had a lot to figure out. Her phone was loaded with apps that would help her with things like basic Japanese and how to get from the airport to Kyoto. However, she wasn't sure which apps would work without an internet connection, so she stored information and directions multiple times in many different formats.

What she had been dreading was learning the local subway system at what would be for her some unknown sleep-deprived hour. There would be at least four different train changes to contend with. All of this while battling exhaustion and hoping her headache wouldn't return. Emily was about to confront the Japanese rail system when the thought occurred to her that she should check with the airport shuttle service. Before leaving to Japan, she had called a Kansai airport shuttle service to arrange a ride to her hotel, but no one understood English. She filled out an online form to notify the shuttle company of her name and arrival time, but never received a confirmation.

She walked to the counter and told them her name, Emily Diane Patrick. A man paged through several printouts on a clipboard and stopped at one. She saw that his finger was pointing to her name. She gasped with relief.

"That's me," she smiled, and almost wanted to cry with elation.

The man nodded and motioned her to follow him. She was led to a white minivan and given a hot wet towel to clean her hands and face. The tingling sensation on her cheeks was as euphoric as the thought that she could sit back and take a nap as the monumental problem of finding her hotel had been solved for her. Several other passengers boarded the shuttle. After credit cards were swiped, they were off to their respective destinations. Just as Emily had made note of landing on an island in the middle of Osaka Bay, she was aware of that she was on the longest two-tier bridge in the world as her eyelids became heavy. She thought of the song by Coldplay that makes mention of the Osaka sun, and wished it hadn't been dark outside.

She was the last person to be dropped off. The driver helped her with her carryon, softly putting it down on the sidewalk. Emily thanked him and pulled out a long handle, wheeling the case through the hotel entrance. A nervous man behind the counter bowed, smiling, maintaining eye contact, presenting her with a hotel booklet and keys with both hands. Emily knew to also receive everything with both hands, returning the consideration and kindness. Once inside her tiny hotel room, she turned on the television, flipping through the channels containing silly game shows and other programming strange to western eyes. This was all she ever wanted. Her dream had been realized. She was in Japan. She fell asleep with a smile.

The next day, she had a cold breakfast at the hotel and went to the convenience store to buy a bento box to pack as a lunch for later. When she paid for it, her change was given to her with a smile and both hands. This politeness lasted a week through her excursions to the many shrines and temples, and lunches at ramen shops, her strolls through parks and bamboo forests. Her subway rides were in trains that were so quiet, it seemed that no matter how many people were crammed together; no one ever talked or made a sound. Kyoto was as calm as she had hoped it would be, peaceful and dreamy like a Hayao

Miyazaki movie. She kept thinking of that scene from Spirited Away when the phantom train traversed a silent sea, the little girl sitting next to her monster friend.

Emily even visited the International Manga Museum and spent a day there admiring the imaginary characters and illustrated worlds. After absorbing the beauty of Kyoto for five days, the ancient imperial palace, Shinto and Buddhist places of worship, the Gion district with women dressed in kimonos and some as geisha and maiko, Emily became anxious with the idea of her vacation coming to an end. She had researched and prepared for her trip to Japan. She knew not to tip, understood the customs and was well aware that very few Japanese people spoke English. What she had not prepared for was going back to America.

In Japan, she felt as if she had been in the one place that suited her in this world. Her shyness was nothing odd in a country where everyone seemed shy. Her inclination to be silent was satisfied to the uttermost. But back she would go. She didn't have a visa for a long-term stay. She had a job and responsibilities back home.

Emily cried the last night in her hotel room, and then went out one final time to explore Central Kyoto after dark. She went to see the Yasaka Shrine, and stood before the large red Ro-mon gate protected from evil spirits by Korean lion-dogs made of stone. The shrine honored a mythological god that defeated a giant eight-headed serpent. And that's what the challenges of her life seemed like to her, large ugly serpents. She stared at the gate and thought hard, asking herself if there was any possible way she could stay in Japan.

She realized that even if she could learn the language, she would forever be an outcast. Being accepted into a group of co-workers or friends that drank beer together after work would be quite difficult. Even spouses are traditionally excluded from any event that is part of a social circle, whether it is parties or business conferences. If, however, she learned Japanese, found work and somehow were accepted into a social group, she would have the greatest friends anyone could have, people that would help and care for her more than even relatives. Perhaps, she mused, this would serve as a secret fantasy she could hold on to for life.

And then there was the color of her skin. Being black would get Emily a lot of stares, but there didn't seem to be any racism in Japan, just shyness. She had once been told that inside of every Japanese person was a friendly soul dying to talk to a foreigner. But how could bonds ever develop if she was the same way? She usually preferred to be around animals and special needs children. She was so sensitive in fact that the slightest things would overwhelm her—the sound of silverware clanging on plates, the possibility of a large gathering of humans. She had always craved going to a place that was absent of noise and where she could be among people that could appreciate her timid ways. She had steered her life towards this journey to silence, but never had she planned for or even considered what she would do when it was time to leave her dream destination and return to a place of overwhelming sound.

The lion-dogs guarding the gate, known as a Komainu, were grotesque and yet beautiful. Emily studied the head of one of the statues intently, the eyes, meant to be terrifying, eliciting a response of fascination. Although she was shy, she was not naturally fearful. Fear was something that children felt in the dark. Emily was always well informed about her surroundings, mature and more curious about things than apprehensive. The Komainu, for some reason, felt like a reflection in a mirror. She thought of it as what she was inside, something enigmatic that she had always hidden. Perhaps it was the strong emotions that she tried to repress. Would she be able to hide them much longer? She wondered. No doubt, it would be painful to tear herself away from the heavenly serenity of Kyoto.

The day of her departure, she slowly made her way back to Osaka, secretly wishing that a Japanese man would fall in love with her and somehow protect and save an angel from falling out of the sky. There was one tall gentleman that helped her purchase subway tickets from a metro vending machine, depositing her Yen and pushing the right buttons. His smile melted her heart. As with all the other people, he bowed and handed her the ticket with both hands. He kept looking at her as she passed the turnstile, and then waved goodbye with an even bigger smile. If only he knew English—if only she had known more Japanese, she thought.

Emily felt less discomfort on the fourteen hour return flight than the first one. There was no thirst or headache this time, or any physical unease. However there was a spiritual distress consuming her heart, aggravated considerably by the passenger seated in front of her that kept violently scratching his right ear with the palm of his hand. He did this so hard that she could actually hear his ear canal squeaking.

She found these sounds disturbing.

She arrived in JFK to layover in New York before boarding another flight that would take her home to Fort Lauderdale, Florida. When she greeted the customs officer, a brawny man in a uniform with his sleeves rolled up to exhibit his tattooed biceps, he glanced at her and her passport and declaration form. He typed something into a computer and then handed Emily back her passport with one hand. No smile. No eye contact.

"Welcome home," he said dispassionately.

She received her passport, taking it with both hands as if she were still in Japan. What the customs officer couldn't have known was that at that very moment he had broken her heart. In Emily's mind, she was now trapped in a society that didn't care for her. The expressions of kindness, the exchanging of things with both hands, the bows to make a person feel special and honored—these sentiments had been replaced by flippant glances and casual transactions that were as mundane as disposable packaging.

Emily felt a weight in her chest and even found it hard to breathe. Never had there been any breakup, disappointment or rejection that had hurt as much. She knew if she were to tell anyone about this, they would probably laugh at her. How could anyone understand what it felt like for someone such as her to find paradise and then to lose it?

She went to an airport shop to purchase bottled water. Again, there was no smile, not the slightest indication that the cashier cared that she was alive. The dismissive returning of change and the expression, have a nice day, were like mourners pouring dirt upon her as she lay in her grave. She went and sat at one of the gates to wait for her flight to Fort Lauderdale, thumbing through a Japanese manga on her phone. She felt her lips quiver with a melancholy she didn't think she would ever be able to recover from.

When it was time for her final flight, she handed the gate attendant her boarding pass with both hands, extending the Japanese custom as long as she could. She resumed reading her digital manga, a story about tiny supernatural luminous beings that enter people through their ears. She remembered a passenger sitting in front her and the repulsive sounds he had made. And then she began to wonder if the man had been infected with some type of worm-like creature that had crawled into his head. The manga seemed to make this absurd fantasy come to life. She thought about what unusual thing she might have also brought back with her from Japan.

She turned off her phone and stared out the window. The sky became dark and her mind went over the volumes of now useless trivia about things one should know when visiting Japan. Her mental chatter turned into a dream without experiencing the other sleep stages first. Normally, it takes a person over an hour to dream, but Emily could close her eyes and instantly be flying or falling or talking to imaginary people. In her dream, she made love to the Japanese man who had helped her at the metro vending machine. We missed our chance in real life, he kept saying. She awoke, heartbroken again.

When she arrived at Fort Lauderdale–Hollywood International Airport the steamy air touched her body as if a soulless leviathan had breathed on her. She took a cab home and slept an entire day before going back to work. Within a week, her co-workers began to notice that she was acting strange. She spoke of creatures hiding in the shadows, adamant that no one could see them because they were invisible to our world. When people would ask if she was all right, she would tell them that she no longer wanted to participate in reality. She only wished to observe it from a distance.

Emily drew lion-dogs in a sketchbook, each time making the eyes and teeth more frightening, miles it seemed from the admin tools on her computer screen that needed to be attended to. Her closest friend, a young woman in the cubicle next to her, became concerned that Emily might be unable to perform her duties as a webcasting coordinator. Every event required careful attention to detail. Registration and listen pages needed to be created to the requirements of the client. Her coworker picked up the slack for a few days, at first thinking that Emily was simply jetlagged, but eventually wondering if something traumatic had happened to her in Japan.

"If I draw something it will come alive," Emily would say.

"So why are you drawing scary monsters?" her coworker would ask.

"They're not monsters. They're foo dogs. They'll protect me."

"Protect you from what?"

Emily would cover her ears and close her eyes.

In early December, Emily took a day off from work one Thursday to drive down to the convention center in Miami Beach. Art Basel week had begun and Emily was eager to explore the exhibits, hoping to stumble upon the work of Asian artists. She encountered vast amounts of western art that she did not care for, walking for hours hoping to find hints of Japan, China or Korea. Discouraged and needing to sit down and rest her feet, she found a seat in a small auditorium that was practically hidden behind the hundreds of galleries in the large arena sized building.

A Russian artist stood before a screen speaking into a microphone. He was tall and thin with wiry gray hair. The slideshow of his work featured miniature houses that he had built and photographed. Each house looked as if it had been shelled by artillery fire. He said he would give a brief talk that day and interviewed in-depth by the chief editor of an art magazine on the following day. When he revealed that the subject matter of his work represented the death of the imagination in a practical world, Emily sat up and listened to his words with great interest. What mainly captivated her was his statement that there was too much noise in life.

Emily looked up his name on her phone and found a website devoted to his work, then an email address. She sent him a quick message thanking him for his thoughtfulness and creativity. She told him that she felt much like one of his model houses and that she too didn't like noise. He was unaware that she was doing this, typing and glancing at him, and then picking up her small backpack and walking away, looking back several times.

While she was still in the convention center, she received a reply from him. He explained to her that there was an existential battle raging inside of her. He asked her if she would like to meet him that evening at a gathering for people who all struggled with the same feelings of not fitting in with the rest of the world. There were of course many elegant cocktail parties in Miami that night to commemorate the start of the art fair, but he knew both of them would obviously prefer not to have that type of commotion. She agreed.

The following morning, Emily's lifeless body was found in a park not far from her home. The pages of her sketchbook had been torn out and scattered around her. Lion-dogs lamenting the stillness of the night.

# CHAPTER TWO

## The Day After

One uniformed police officer photographed the scene while an investigator in a jumpsuit collected the drawings with tweezers, putting them into zip lock bags. Detectives Salter and Ramos approached Emily's naked body as if it were a soundless requiem mass. Soul stirring music that felt just out of reach of human ears seemed to linger over her. As Detective Ryan Salter squatted next to Emily, he gave his partner, rookie detective Kim Ramos, a look as if to convey the uniqueness of this tragic discovery. Ramos had never seen Salter look so sadly into the eyes of the deceased before.

Salter took the badge that had been dangling from a chain around his neck and tapped it on his mouth as if to help him better think.

"They called this in as a possible overdose?" Salter said. "It's obviously not an overdose."

"Obviously," said the man collecting evidence.

"Marks around the neck," said Detective Ramos.

The man pulled back one eyelid. "Petechial hemorrhage. It's hard to see. You have to get close."

Salter leaned closer to see the tiny markings of broken blood vessels in the eye.

"That and a slight redness under the eyes," the man said.

Salter stood and adjusted his suit and tie as well as the ID tag clipped to his lapel. He spoke softly to Ramos. "Do you feel it?"

Ramos nodded.

They had recently discussed rare cases in which there was a

tangible sense of something collapsing inward in the air, an indication, perhaps, that there was nothing ordinary about the person they would be considering.

Emily's micro braids and dark porcelain skin glimmered in the morning light. Salter felt almost unworthy to be witnessing the falling of an angel to earth.

"Who would want to kill such a beautiful girl?" Salter muttered almost to himself.

Ramos shook her head.

"So what do we know?" Salter asked.

The man in the jumpsuit clasped his latex gloved hands together and then held them far apart to indicate that the crime scene encompassed the visible area before them. "Her purse, cell phone—all her belongings are right here. Her car registration indicates that the gold Nissan parked nearby is hers."

"You already went through her wallet?" Ramos asked.

"Carefully. We still have to dust every card and bill as well as her body. It's time consuming to pick up the drawings without damaging them too much. The dew on the grass makes the ink drawings bleed a little when you try to move them. At least there's no breeze this morning. I'm doing DNA and searching for residues and fibers."

"What's her name?" Salter asked.

"Emily Diane Patrick, according to her Florida driver's license—twenty four years old.

"Someone killed her—tore all these pages out of a drawing book and tossed them all over the place," Salter said. "Nobody heard or saw anything?"

"An officer drove by and spotted her."

"I'll knock on a few doors and ask around," Ramos said.

"I think we can solve this," Salter said. "We have her phone. Her entire life is in there."

"Good."

"We usually get lucky," Salter tightened his forehead. "Someone turns someone in or we find out something by accident. But this time we have a treasure trove of evidence."

"So we'll prioritize this case as likely to be solved."

"Let's do that. The next couple of days, we live and breathe and think about nothing except Emily Patrick."

Within the hour, detectives Salter and Ramos had copied all the information on Emily's phone with cellular seizure investigation sticks and were scrolling through her personal photos on their laptops. They remained at the crime scene for several hours and then went back to the station to comb through the information in the comfort of their offices, considerably cooler than a humid South Florida day in December.

They had found nothing in the lion-dog drawings except her initials, EDP, written into a tiny box on the bottom of each page. There was nothing remarkable about her other belongings. Her purse and clothes showed no signs of struggle. Early indications were that there was no rape or sexual assault. Evidence had been put into boxes along with the cell phone after the only fingerprints found on it were determined to belong to Emily.

"She'd recently been to Japan," Salter said looking at a full screen photo.

"I can see that," Ramos said. "She took a lot of selfies. This one is so cute. She wore a kimono. I wonder if she got it at a 24 hour kimono rental place-"

Salter familiarized himself with Emily's cell phone which had not been locked. She was still logged into her Yahoo mail. Her correspondences seemed to offer the most promising glimpse into her life.

"Here's her flight itinerary from Travelocity," he said. "Looks like she spent one week in Kyoto."

"I wonder why so few days," she said. "To make such an incredibly long trip—it seems like you would need a couple of weeks to make it worth it."

"Maybe she could only afford one week," he said. "She got a pretty good deal."

"That's still one hell of a long trip for only a week."

"She probably had the time of her life. How many people can say they've been to Japan?"

"I've been," she smiled.

"You've been all over," he sighed. "You're part Asian-"

"Half Filipino," she said.

Salter continued to thumb through Emily's emails. "I'm mixed too. My mother is half Cuban."

"I know," she said. "You told me. And I told you that you reminded me of the US Olympic swimmer—the one with the Cuban mom."

"Because we have the same first name?"

"You look a little like him too."

"Don't compare me with him. I'm not that good looking."

"Sure you are."

"I'm going to tell your husband that you're hitting on me," Salter laughed.

Ramos narrowed her eyes. "When are you going to get married so I can have long talks with your wife?"

"Never."

"Ever heard that Eagles' song—you better let somebody love you before it's too late?" she sang the lyrics.

"Too late? What's going to happen?"

"You'll grow old and lonely."

Salter brooded with interest, bringing the phone closer to his face. "I should've started with her most recent messages. Last night someone named Simeon Suslov sent her this. Let me read it to you: Thank you, Emily, for taking the time to write to me. I'm flattered by your kind words and happy that you were somehow able to make a connection to the things I spoke about. I believe there is an existential battle raging inside of you, the type that I am well familiar with. You certainly have the heart of an artist. I too wish there were more Asian art at the fair. Perhaps it is some extraordinary coincidence, but I'm going to a Japanese event of sorts tonight. It's for people like us who don't seem to fit in with the rest of the world. I would be honored if you were to come tonight. Do you think you can make it?"

"And what was her response?"

Salter selected and read the last message that Emily would ever receive. "He sent her an address and directions. So, I guess she said yes. Wait—let me go into the sent folder. I'm dying to see what she wrote him."

"I have a lot of questions for this Simeon guy," Ramos said.

"You and me both," Salter said. "The last message says: Thank you. I would love to go. Let's see what the first message she wrote him says-"

"Can't trust anyone," Ramos said.

"Okay, here it is: Mr. Suslov. I just googled you and found your email on your website. As I write this, I'm here at Art Basel, listening to you speak. I suppose I should be paying attention, but I just wanted to express my gratitude. I recently returned from Kyoto. I'm so lost. I wish I were back in Japan. I feel much like one of your model houses. I think you know what I mean. Your work is pure genius, by the way. And I too don't like noise. Thank you for lifting my spirit."

"What's his name again?"

"Simeon Suslov."

Ramos typed his name into a search engine and navigated to the official Simeon Suslov website. "He's being interviewed today at Art Basel."

"Ever been?" Salter asked.

"Never," Ramos replied.

"I've always wanted to go. I'd like to hear what Mr. Suslov has to say in his interview before we question him. Let's immerse ourselves in his world."

"Do you think the interviewer will ask him if he has recently committed murder?"

"I doubt it," Salter smiled. "All right, we should notify next of kin within 24 to 48 hours. We need to visit her apartment, talk to co-workers—so much to do. I'll get Hector to go over the physical evidence. But this Simeon guy comes first."

Salter and Ramos made the one hour drive down to the Miami Beach Convention Center, entering the world's most ostentatious art fair and moving past the throngs of art enthusiasts. There were many eccentrics dressed as if they might be undiscovered artists screaming for attention among the thousands of exhibited artists from over thirty countries. The two detectives were surprised to find the auditorium so quickly among the two hundred or so exhibitors. They just happened to make several correct turns in the maze of galleries and found themselves at a small auditorium with about one hundred chairs.

On the stage were an elderly Czech artist and his interpreter. The interviewer, a heavy British man, spoke expressively with his hands, bellowing out the Queen's English. "Can you please elaborate on this concept of utopia in your work?" he said pompously.

"That's not him," Ramos whispered.

"I don't think so," Salter replied.

The Czech man spoke for a while in his native tongue, and then his interpreter relayed the sentiment that the question was irrelevant.

"Yes," the interviewer snapped back. "But tell me something of this concept of utopia and how it relates to your work."

Again, the Czech spoke at length, and then the interpreter expressed his desire to elude the question by describing his childhood and the beatings he endured by his father.

After the interview ended, Salter and Ramos waited for Simeon Suslov in the once again empty auditorium.

"I'm not sure I understand art," Salter said.

"That interview sure took a lot of the magic out of it," Ramos said.

"What magic?" he said. "I saw a large blank canvas with a single pencil mark in the center of it selling for over seventy thousand dollars. How is that art? What's so magical about it? I could have done that."

"You could have, but you're not well connected in the art world," she smiled.

"This is a freak show," he said. "Did you see that guy with all the pipes and things coming out of his head?"

"I did. I did."

Within twenty minutes, the auditorium darkened and seats filled again. A tall man appeared before the large curved wall painted by the light from a projection. He sat down, making no attempt to hide that he was admiring the beauty of the woman who was to interview him, the editor of a prestigious art magazine. She wore an elegant black dress with a low cut neckline.

He played with his silver hair. It was curly in a way that seemed to defy gravity, a little like Einstein's hair. His face was sun burnt from spending his days at the boat yard working on his yacht. He lifted his eyebrows, making subtle gestures intended to seduce.

"Today I have the honor of introducing to you renown avant-garde artist, Simeon Suslov," the editor said.

The audience clapped. Suslov nodded in appreciation. A slide of a model house appeared on the screen.

"Spectacular work," she said. "It's almost otherworldly. What wonderful metaphors and what a voracious yearning for clarity and bold visual language. Can you talk a little about this work, the process involved, and if this can be replicated in perpetuity?"

Simeon Suslov playfully stuck out his lower lip and then sighed. "Yes and no. I suppose it could go on forever. But it is not the same as the first impression you have. It's like when a man sees a beautiful woman. Before thought or emotion, just as the signal is leaving the retina and entering the brain, there is a spark of something. Who can say what it is? It's like that dress you're wearing. Just like the air, it separates us. Yet this cruel object is exquisite, but nothing without a beautiful person inside of it. And the beautiful person is nothing without the beauty within."

"So it's about impressions," she smiled.

"What is real? To one person, life is wonderful, to another it's hell. How can I know what the truth is? I'm not omniscient. Who can best interpret a holy book, or a constitution, or a theory of art? None of us are God. And what is art? What is it? Perhaps that's too big a question. I'm not good with absolutes. Let's simplify. What is art as it relates to me? Much easier question, don't you think? Me—my life—my art. Hmm. My life is just a product of my own perceptions. However, today I want to be very candid. I'd like to tell my own personal truth, or at least what I recall as experience. I'll talk about myself, only then can you understand my art."

"Yes, please tell us about yourself."

"Jonathon."

"Jonathon?"

"Jonathon was an executive at a brokerage house. He was quite brilliant. He actually predicted the rise of China, India and Brazil. Everyone could tell he would be very successful one day. But of course, he was no match for his own life. He was too capable, too talented. Eventually he got sucked in by the power and money. He lost his soul. He accumulated an atrocious amount of wealth in junk bonds and money laundering. He threw lavish parties where he could associate with other wealthy bankers obsessed with cocaine and excess and chasing after more and more and more—Five homes and private jets, it's never enough. But—he's one of the ones that got caught in the end. He fled to Indonesia. They almost tracked him down, but then he fled somewhere else where they finally nailed him.

"We were once roommates in college. We made an agreement that if one of us should ever fall into great fortune, that we would help the other. He didn't need to make that pact with me. His father was a wealthy man. But perhaps he had meant super wealth all along. At any rate, because of the pact, one night as he was casually snorting lines of cocaine with his art dealer, he mentioned my name. Sure, the man said, we'll make him a big name in the art world. And just like that, the market value of my artwork skyrocketed. My fan base now consists of the ultra-rich. Not bad, huh?"

"Are you sure you want to go on?" the editor asked.

"Of course."

"This isn't good," she covered her microphone and whispered. "You're committing career suicide."

"Don't worry," Suslov winked. "So back to my friend, Jonathon. You could say that I was very lucky to know him. Since then, I've met many honorable bankers and art dealers. The art world is not corrupt for the most part. But sometimes it takes some sort of transgression or something dark and almost criminal for things to happen. Just like politicians—they've got to be devious to out-maneuver and destroy their enemies. Or like the parable of the shrewd manager—the guy who is deceitful is praised in the end. So it is with these little model houses. They appear damaged, pock-marked by war. But what does that represent? It's like when you dream. Nothing is what it seems. Every object within the dream is a symbol—a profound, fanciful symbol. Why and how is the subconscious mind so ingenious? Back to my point, the damaged houses are a symbol for damaged people. This is the agonizing truth about life. The people living on this planet are filled with pain and loneliness. Why? Because everyone plays by the rules. People are too shy to admit they're lonely—too shy to admit that they feel like complete failures. And why are they failures? Because the world isn't fair."

The editor tilted her head with interest. "Could the damaged houses literally represent broken homes? Is this a grand unifying theory of the human condition?"

"We are social creatures after all," Suslov said. "We crave intimacy, but we're unsure how to achieve it. We want to love and be loved, but who can really open themselves up and reveal all that is dark and painful? People enter into the institution of marriage, but do they really know the person they share their lives with? Sometimes those are the loneliest people of all. But there are also the ones that don't even feel like they belong in this world. Imagine those who are very artistic and sensitive, whether they express it or not—imagine what it is like for them to always want to withdraw into their own worlds. They don't want to be in the painting. They simply want to observe it, appreciate the beauty, movement, form and color. The world is simply too overwhelming, too noisy. They want to turn down the sound and watch it like a silent movie. Have you ever known anyone like that?"

"Have I ever known anyone like that?" the editor repeated the question. "I suppose writing about art can be like that for me. I enjoy critiquing more than I would creating."

"And what of pain and loneliness?"

The editor darted her eyes around. "We all have our moments. Why don't you tell us more from your personal experience-"

"I didn't expect you to feel comfortable answering that question," Suslov smiled. "Back in college around the time I knew Jonathon the executive, I had no artistic inclination whatsoever. I was just a young man, the grandson of a Russian that came to America right after the October Revolution. Where they got the money to send me off to school, I don't know. However, school was not the great challenge of my life. My mind was. I had begun a descent into madness. I somehow knew that I needed to hide my mental illness from others. If I were to be institutionalized, that would be the end of me. During a period of many months, I felt my sanity slipping away. I heard voices and saw things that could not be explained logically. I intuitively sensed that I was getting very close to a thin boundary that separated our world from another world. And one day, I touched that other world. After that, I felt peace and became a very different person."

"What kind of person did you become?"

"I became an artist and a healer—someone that could sense pain in others. People immediately felt that they could confide in me, admit things to me. They would feel better just being around me. And I became interested in creative expression. I wanted to communicate the many things that I was feeling."

"What exactly did you see when you touched this other world?"

"I cannot tell you with words, but I've never forgotten it. It is not only fuel for the imagination—it has left a mark on me, making me something…rather odd. Perhaps you've been getting a sense of this. I do want to say that there is so much more going on than we realize."

"I kind of like this guy," Salter whispered to Ramos. "I hope he's not our killer."

# CHAPTER THREE

After the interview, Simeon Suslov and the editor continued to talk amongst themselves as people were leaving the auditorium. Salter and Ramos approached, walking on to the stage with disarming smiles.

The editor noticed them and ended the conversation. "Looks like you have people that want to talk to you." As she stood to leave, a momentary look of disappointment flashed across Suslov's face. Then he turned to look at the two detectives and greeted them with a warm expression.

"Mr. Suslov, we're detectives from Fort Lauderdale," Ramos said. "Can we ask you a few questions?"

"Certainly," Suslov said. "Does this have to do with my friend Jonathon?"

"No," Salter said. "But that was an interesting talk you gave. So it really is about who you know."

"Sometimes it is," Suslov said.

"I hope we didn't chase away your friend," Salter said.

"Not at all. An old man like me is just happy to make conversation, even if it's brief. So what can I do for you? Is everything okay?"

"Unfortunately, there is a very serious matter we would like to talk to you about," Ramos said.

"Can we go outside where it's quieter?" Salter asked. "We don't want to drag you all the way to Fort Lauderdale. Maybe we can find a nice spot to talk for a while."

The three walked out of the auditorium. "Yes, of course—has something happened?" Suslov asked.

"It's about someone you were corresponding with via email yesterday," Ramos said. "Emily Patrick."

"Emily—yes—Emily. Is she okay?"

They went out the double exit doors, squinting in the sun. Salter and Ramos put on sunglasses.

"Did you get to meet her?" Salter asked.

"Yes, I did. Is she okay? Please tell me."

"I'm afraid not," Salter said.

"Oh my God," Suslov turned pale.

"You wouldn't want to grab a bite with us?"

"I suppose. Tell me, what happened to Emily?"

"She was found dead this morning," Ramos said.

Suslov staggered for a moment, seemingly losing his balance.

"Let's have lunch—our treat," Salter said.

"I think I've lost my appetite," Suslov said.

Salter drove them down Washington Street until they saw a Cuban restaurant. They were seated at a table for four, surrounded by paintings of the Viñales Valley. Salter and Ramos both ordered medianoche sandwiches.

"Can you please tell us about last night?" Salter asked.

"She's really dead?" Suslov asked.

"Yes, she is," Ramos said.

"How did she die?"

"We're still trying to determine that."

Suslov heaved a long sigh. "Just to make sure we're talking about the same person—beautiful young black girl with thin braids, right?"

"That's her," Salter said.

Ramos held out her phone with a picture of Emily's face as they had found her in the park.

"It is her," Suslov said with a note of heartbreak.

"It is," Ramos said.

"Am I a suspect? Do I need a lawyer?"

"We're just asking questions," Salter said. "You could be a very big help to us in finding out what happened last night. Will you help us?"

"I'll tell you everything I know."

Salter and Ramos both put their hands together and leaned slightly forward.

"You must have seen the email that I responded to," Suslov said. "That's why you want to talk to me. Emily seemed like someone that was hurting—lonely, discouraged, overwhelmed by life. And, like myself, a lover of Asian art. I told her about a gathering in the evening…What I'm about to tell you is going to violate people's private lives. Do you understand?"

"Understood," Salter said.

"I'm sure you've heard of secret societies," Suslov said.

"Secret societies? What—like the Illuminati?" Ramos asked.

"Yes," came Suslov's sad smile. "Like that."

"So it was a secret society that you invited Emily to—why?" Salter asked.

"It's called The Hermetic Order of the Mystic Koyosha," Suslov said softly. "It's based on ancient Samurai legends. We're all lovers of Japan, among other things."

"What are the other things?" Ramos asked.

"What you have to understand is that secret societies are not some amalgamation of shady people bent on world domination," Suslov said. "There comes a time that you want to be around friends that can keep secrets. It's not because we're hiding anything dark or illicit. Let me explain. If you've used social media for any amount of time, it soon becomes apparent that opinions are not welcomed. The moment you express an opinion, you're attacked and condemned by half the people that are your supposed friends or followers or whatever you want to call them. A lot of the people in our group are important people that can't risk alienating half the public. Community leaders, heads of philanthropic organizations, all sorts of people, even church pastors. Just imagine you're heading a congregation and knowing that if you were to even question the doctrine of your particular denomination it might lead to the board of elders extending to you the left foot of fellowship—the pink slip—excommunication."

"I don't mean to sound rude," Salter said. "But why do you belong to a secret society? You're not an important community leader. In fact, since you're an artist, wouldn't people simply assume that they could guess your politics and worldview? —unless you're hiding something very personal that you can only share with a few people."

"We all have something to hide. If you heard the interview today, you might remember that I spoke about a crisis I went through when I was young. I don't know if I should tell you this because a girl died yesterday and right now I don't want to appear like a raging psychopath or someone that would hurt another person."

"You seem fine to me," Salter said.

"I struggled with mental illness as a young man. Most people that go through what I went through are either locked away or given powerful drugs. Luckily, I came out of it. Most aren't so fortunate. I think that when someone is on the verge of progressing spiritually or attaining a higher level of consciousness, they sometimes go through a difficult period. They might think they're going crazy. In a way, they *are* going crazy. Looking back, I realize that it was a sign that I had encountered the world of the mystical and paranormal."

"Is that why it's called the order of the mystic something?" Ramos asked.

"The Hermetic Order of the Mystic Koyosha," Suslov corrected her.

"So you're a mystic," Ramos said.

"Sort of."

"Every religion has a mystical branch," Salter said. "Isn't that right? Buddhism has Zen, Islam has Sufism, Judaism has Kabbalah, Christianity has the Contemplatives-"

"For the most part, I think you are correct," Suslov said. "But mysticism can't be explained with words. Most people wouldn't understand it, so it's only for the few. Besides, people have a tendency towards turning things into religions or cults. Anyway, the Koyosha went far beyond mysticism. We were in tune with the other side."

"The other side—what do you mean by that?" Salter asked.

Suslov was quiet for a moment before responding. "We like to tell each other ghost stories."

"Ghost stories—like stuff that people have seen with their own eyes?" Ramos asked.

"We tell two kinds of stories. Things we experience and the make-believe. The make-believe stories give us a certain level of comfort in revealing things that may be difficult to share with others. We disguise the truth with lots of fantasy." Suslov paused to look at a painting of the Viñales Valley. "It's strange to talk about ghosts, knowing that Emily is dead. You have no idea how she died? Could it have been suicide?"

Salter sadly shook his head. "Did she seem suicidal?"

"I thought she was having a great time last night," Suslov said. "I saw her smiling."

"She had recently been to Japan," Salter said. "She must have been happy to be a part of something with a Japanese theme. You said your society was based on Samurai legends?"

"The Mystic Koyosha was inspired by a Japanese order that wanted to return to the days of special privileges for the Samurai class. However, we are mostly interested in the rituals. Last night, we had an initiation. We told stories and blew out candles."

"Why was this invitation to join a secret society extended to Emily?" Ramos asked. "She wasn't an important figure in the community. Was it because she was having a crisis like the one you had?"

"That's precisely the reason," Suslov said. "I had a strong sense that she was going through a very difficult time. I did a background check on her. When we met at the Mystic Koyosha, I asked a few questions just to be sure she fit in with the rest of us."

Ramos wrinkled her forehead. "What did you ask her?"

"I just asked her one question designed to get her to open up to me—tell me about yourself. I learned about her trip to Kyoto and how much she missed being there. I understand how it can affect one's mood to be on vacation one moment and return to work right after that. You spend days utterly free, enjoying life, and suddenly you wake up and life is normal and uninteresting again. Some people are more depressed than others after they travel, but this was something completely different. She told me about strange luminous creatures entering her brain through her ear canal. She thought that other passengers on her plane had also returned from Japan with wormlike beings in their ears. In Shinto religion in Japan there are spirits called kami that are said to manifest themselves as rocks, plants or animals, just about anything including people. Emily seemed to have kami nature. Not just because she thought she had something in her ears, but also because she wanted to be like a spirit, invisible and not stuck at a job and having to talk to others. She craved silence and stillness. She said, however, that the creatures in her ears were absorbing some of the noise of this world, and she thought that perhaps that wasn't a bad thing."

"And what did you think of that?" Ramos asked.

"I thought she was losing her mind," Suslov said with sad amusement. "Exactly the kind of person that might be ready for the Mystic Koyosha."

"You didn't think that she needed psychological counseling?"

Ramos asked.

"I'm not against that," Suslov said. "But I simply thought she could use some friends. And if she were truly going through something similar to what I went through, then she was essentially among family now. I might even be able to make the transition into her next stage in life less painful."

"I'm sure you were also noticed that she was a beautiful young woman," Salter said.

"I was."

"When you were being interviewed today, you were quite enamored with the woman in the low cut dress. You even seemed to be flirting with her. Was it anything like that with Emily?"

Suslov gave the detectives a look of disappointment. "No. Emily was experiencing something dark and painful. I felt very sympathetic towards her. I admit that I like the company of attractive women, but I know when to treat someone like a daughter or sister. I understood her better than she could ever have imagined. I wanted her to be happy. I was grateful for the opportunity to bring a little bit of Japan back into her life."

The medianoches arrived. The pork and ham sandwiches warmed in a press made Salter's palette tingle. He lifted the triangular edge of one of the egg dough halves and inhaled the aroma.

"The best thing about this is the mustard," Salter said. "Sure you don't want my other half?"

"I'm not hungry," Suslov said. "I guess you're use to these things, but I'm too upset about Emily to eat.

"It's tragic," Salter said. "But we have to eat. So, she shows up and tells you about creatures in her ears. What else did she have to say?"

"She told me how much she loved art," Suslov said. "She even showed me her drawing book. It had quite a few renderings of Chinese foo dogs. There were some dragons and a few other things. She asked me what it would take to be an artist. Apparently she hated her job and just wanted the kind of work where she never needed to talk to anyone."

"Can you explain the foo dogs?" Ramos asked.

"Foo dogs, lion-dogs—I'm not sure what the difference is between the Komainu and Chinese guardian lions. But I think it's all basically to ward off evil spirits. The males usually have their paws on top of a globe to symbolize dominance. As far as Emily was concerned, the drawings may have been a way to make herself feel safer. This existential crisis she was going through must have been a very frightening ordeal for her. No one would ever understand unless they went through it themselves."

Salter removed a pickle from his sandwich and put it on Ramos' plate.

"You don't like pickles?" Ramos asked.

"Depends," Salter said. "The tanginess of the mustard is just right. It doesn't need pickles."

"I thought you were Cuban."

"Half—remember? Sure I can't get you anything, Mr. Suslov?"

"No, thank you," Suslov said. "You can call me Simeon."

"All right, Simeon," Salter said. "Tell us everything that happened at the gathering last night from the beginning to the very last time you saw Emily."

Suslov picked up his glass of water sipped from it as if it were vodka, helping him to forget the things he was about to remember. He furrowed his brow, bit his lip and faintly shook his head with sorrow. Then he recounted Emily's last night.

# CHAPTER FOUR

## The Night of the Murder

At twilight, Emily pulled up in her gold Nissan. The security guard had buzzed her into the gated community, her name on a list of guests expected at the home of Federico Carlesimo Jafet. She found the address among the many elegant homes and gleaming lakes and tropical landscaping. Parking her car in front of the large estate, she checked her phone again to make sure she had the correct house number. She wasn't sure if she should bring her backpack which was almost small enough to be a purse, but not elegant enough for a formal event. The chance that her drawings might come up in a conversation made it seem necessary to bring it. So she brought the backpack along, almost as a security object containing art, the language of the mystics.

At the grand entry door, Emily softly knocked, afraid that the doorbell might set off a cacophony of chiming. A dark skinned woman holding a wine glass greeted her.

"Emily?"

"Yes—hi."

"We've been expecting you. There's no one here. Everyone is in the building in the back."

Emily followed the woman through a dimly lit mansion and out the rear. There was a small domed building that looked like a private chapel made out of porous limestone. The doors were made of dark stained mahogany wood with the images of lambs carved into them.

"This is amazing," Emily said.

"It's a reproduction of an ancient church in what was at the time Asia Minor. The walls are about two feet thick. Isn't it beautiful?"

"Stunning."

They walked inside to what looked very much like a two thousand year old place of worship, rows of empty wooden pews under a fresco-covered ceiling. In the dome interior were painted what looked like samurai holding large shields with strange symbols on them. A long chain hung from the highest point, bearing the weight of a large chandelier of blue candles. Towards the back of the building behind two columns was a chancel in the shape of a half circle. There, about eighteen people sat in tall leather chairs making a full circle around a small table. They were talking and laughing, each completely immersed in conversation. As Emily and the other woman approached the group, they noticed two empty chairs, one of them next to Simeon Suslov.

"Are you Emily?" Suslov asked.

"Yes," she smiled. "And I know who you are."

"Please sit you didn't tell me you were such a pretty girl."

"Thank you," she mouthed the words as she sat next to him, the other woman taking the second seat.

Emily was relieved that it wasn't a formal event. It seemed more of a business casual affair. However, she noticed that she was the only one not wearing blue. It wasn't a sea of blue, but it was obvious that everyone had made an attempt to wear at least one item in the Japanese color of calmness and stability. Suslov was more conspicuous in a blue sports coat and jeans.

"Why don't you tell me about yourself," Suslov said.

Emily thought for a moment. "Hmm—I've kind of been in the dumps since I returned from Japan. I wish I could go back. The people are so quiet there. They're so much like me—shy and a little bit strange. I work for a technology company. All I do is talk to angry clients on the phone all day. It's a very complicated service we provide. You have to be a geek, and you have to be a people person. The people part is something I'm not good at. I wish I could just quit my job and get away from everyone. I'm tired of all the rudeness. I've never understood how anyone could be mean. Don't they care about what another person is feeling? It doesn't seem like anyone cares about anyone else. Life is just one big competition. Everyone is looking out for themselves. In Japan, every time I encountered another person, every insignificant transaction was made with a smile and a bow. People would always hand me things with both hands and they would look me in the eyes. I don't know if it's all a façade. I don't know if it's just a custom and they don't really mean any of it or if they care at all, but it sure feels nice. It felt so good when I was there. Since I've been back, you're the only person that seems to care."

"I do," Suslov said. "And I know exactly what you mean."

A man introduced himself as Federico Carlesimo Jafet and told the group not to worry, refreshments would be arriving soon.

"Jafet is a very nice man," Suslov whispered to Emily. "Actually, everyone here is very kind and fairly enlightened. There are quite a few patrons of the arts and philanthropists. You are among people that care deeply about others, about spirituality, poetry—the arts—quite a fascinating bunch. Of course there is no one rich enough to solve the world's problems, but these people are very generous and do much, usually completely anonymously. The Asian man to the right of Jafet is a modern day descendent of one of Japan's oldest feudal dynasties. He participates in the famous Soma Noma-oi festival where they continue to practice the traditions of the Samurai. You truly are among extraordinary people."

"Why did you invite me?" Emily asked.

"Because you're like me," he said. "You may not be a great mover and shaker, but you are at the very threshold of something amazing."

"Amazing? What?"

"As you feel yourself losing your place in this world, you're getting closer and closer to piercing the veil."

"I don't understand," she said.

"Maybe after tonight, you will."

"I wouldn't mind being more like you," she said.

"Why do you say that?" he said.

"How does one become an artist?"

Suslov smiled and sighed. "That's like asking how one becomes a drug addict. Suppose I were to ask myself—what am I going to do about this problem I have? I can't seem to stop drawing, sculpting and painting. I'm exhausted, why can't I stop? My hands hurt. I wish I could take a break from it all. You try but you can't. Oh what a problem. If you have this problem, then you're an artist. Do you have this problem?"

"Maybe a little," she said.

"You're probably an artist."

Emily took her drawing book out of her backpack and handed it to Suslov. He opened it and studied the renderings.

Federico Carlesimo Jafet spoke loudly to get everyone's attention. "All right, you're all here. Let's get started. Obviously we have a guest today."

Emily lifted her hand and gave them a playful smirk.

"Emily Patrick?" Jafet smiled at her.

"That's me," she said.

"Do you, Emily Patrick, of your own free will and accord solemnly and sincerely promise to keep and conceal and never reveal the secrets of The Hermetic Order of the Mystic Koyosha, unless they are a worthy brother or sister of the order?"

"I will," Emily said.

Jafet nodded with contentment. "Simeon, like all of us, has the discretion of inviting someone like you to our gathering. And yet with this privilege, few of us ever find someone worthy enough to bring. So consider yourself special."

"I had a very strong intuition about her," Suslov said. "It was actually quite a powerful feeling I had when I read her message. She emailed me when I was speaking about my work at Art Basel earlier today. Her words jumped out at me as if they were pure spirit. It was like looking into a mirror. I saw so much of myself in her. This is the first time that I've seen her, so no—I didn't invite her here because she's a beautiful woman. I know I have quite a reputation."

The group laughed. Emily smiled and shook her head with amusement.

"Here's the truth about us," Jafet said. "We are a rather odd group of people. We have all decided at some point that we no longer want to be in the world. We simply want to observe and appreciate all its beauty. Some of us, like Simeon, still appreciate the world through the discipline of seeing and creating. But most of us prefer to not exist, and simply travel, explore and observe while drawing little attention to ourselves. We'd rather not be noticed, like spirits moving through nature, without care or concern—not involved in all the human drama."

Emily looked up at the frescos on the ceiling and noticed mountains covered in mist, a solar eclipse and small childlike creatures hiding in trees.

"And so we like this concept of being invisible so much that we tell each other ghost stories. It's sort of something based on a Japanese tradition. Some say that in ancient times, Samurai would tell spooky stories and blow out candles. The light of the candles represent protection from things just beyond our realm of existence. Tonight we will tell four stories. Emily, you will prove your Samurai courage by telling a story and blowing out the last candle. That is your initiation into the The Hermetic Order of the Mystic Koyosha. Once you blow out the last candle and the room is dark, you are one of us. Would you like to do this?"

"Yes," Emily said. "I think I'm already one of you. I just want to be invisible."

"Good," Jafet said. "Let us begin."

A man dressed in a Japanese haori took four blue extra wide pillar candles out of a burlap sack, placed them on the table and lit them. Another person came and wrapped Emily's shoulders in a blue silk shawl and then turned off all the lights to the chapel.

"I'll go first," said Jafet.

"Don't try to think of a story while the others are telling theirs," Suslov whispered. "Just enjoy them and when it's your time to tell one, it will just pour out of you without much thought. Just sit back and listen carefully."

"Usually my stories are inspired by famous Japanese tales," Jafet said. "As most of you know, Japanese ghosts are known as yūrei. I would like to tell you something a little more original tonight. I wonder if you can guess if this yūrei is something out of my imagination or something real that I once experienced. It began shortly after my first wife left me. As I awoke in the morning, I heard a very faint voice saying—go see the baby, but don't commit murder. I didn't need a voice to tell me that. I didn't have the slightest intention of hurting anyone. However, I did go to visit my infant child that evening. I showed up unannounced to her apartment and noticed that the front door wasn't locked. I thought I heard screaming, so I entered only to find the baby sound asleep in one room, and my estranged wife in another room apparently engaging in sex with a man behind a closed door. No wonder she wanted to leave me, I thought. She had fallen in love with someone else. I remembered the voice and vowed not to lose my temper. I stood there for a while, unsure of what to do. I didn't want to wake up the baby. The question was whether or not I was going to barge into the room where all the screaming was coming from and tell my estranged wife what a shameless and despicable person she was. The screaming grew louder and the baby slept—well—like a baby. I heard the most vulgar profanity coursing out of my estranged wife. And then I heard her telling her lover that he was disgusting and repulsive. How can you do this to me? She shrieked. Thoughts were racing through my head—serves her right. But I also entertained the possibility that someone was seriously hurting her and that I should help, no matter how heartbroken I felt. Perhaps, I thought, entering that room would lead to a brawl and ultimately murder. So I stood there frozen, unable to decide what to do. And then I heard her scream, No no no! But soon it stopped. I was shaking with a mixture of emotions—terror, anguish, shock. After a little while, it started again. No! she screamed. No more! My trembling worsened. I went to the baby's room and kissed my child on the head. The sweet scent comforted me for a moment, but then the screaming and pounding sounds grew louder. I thought that perhaps I was imagining things. I heard snorting and growling sounds, almost as if there was an enormous beast in the room. I smelled a musky odor and felt rumbling, sickening vibrations on the floor. I finally went to open the door. I had to know what was happening. For a brief moment, I saw blood splattered all over the walls and carnage everywhere. And then the very next moment I saw my estranged wife, alone, peacefully sleeping in bed in a perfectly spotless room. I saw another woman appear and sit next to her. She was milky white with long disheveled hair. She looked at me and said…this is what happened to me. I just needed someone to know. And then she disappeared. I closed the door and left the apartment. Several days later, my estranged wife called me to apologize. In a rueful voice she admitted that it was the most shameful moment of her life for me to walk in on her while she had been in the throes of passion with her lover. She would never forget the look I gave her. I didn't tell her that I had seen something completely different. And so, to this day, I wonder if perhaps catching her in the act adultery—I considered it to be that—was so painful that I simply repressed it, and now have no memory of it. But there's another possible explanation. The yūrei had provided me an alternate experience to spare me the trauma. A yūrei always wants something. In this instant, someone to empathize with her suffering, to know what happened to her, and someone to help. Having resolved her emotional conflict, the yūrei no longer needed to continue her hauntings and became my protector—such is the way of the yūrei. Every August, she returns to accept my gratitude." Jafet kneeled in front of the table and blew out one blue candle. The room dimmed slightly.

"It really has nothing to do with mysticism," Suslov whispered to Emily. "It's just something he needed to share. I'll explain to you sometime."

The scent of the snuffed out flame reached Emily's nostrils. It carried with it a piece of the story. Did Jafet truly believe that he had a protector beyond the physical plane? Was any of his story true? Nothing mattered as much as the sense Emily felt that the world was full of beings, mysteries and stories. And just as she had felt this, Suslov spoke to her again with delighted eyes.

"A true mystic believes that the creator—the infinite cosmos—is so vast and good that it cannot be adequately expressed or represented by one thing alone. That is why there are so many creatures, beings, and worlds to chronical the splendor of existence. We are many parts, but together we are time itself, we are life itself."

"That's why there are so many things in the world?" she asked.

"Think of all the variety," Suslov said. "So many types of animals and plants-"

"I think there are supernatural creatures in my ears," she said.

"You do?" he asked.

"I just have a strange feeling that there was something on the plane back from Japan. And now there's something in my ears—luminous beings—going into my brain."

Suslov smiled. "Look at what stress had done to you. I think you belong with us."

Someone arrived with red wine to serve to the members of the Mystic Koyosha. Emily looked back at the ceiling, fascinated by the artwork.

"Are those fairies in the trees?" she asked.

"They're Kijimuna," Suslov said. "They look like little children living in the woods. There are all kinds of spirits in Japanese folklore. It is said that some of them have no knowledge of evil, so their hearts never grow old."

"I think I know what story to tell when it's my turn," Emily said.

"Don't think about it, just let the story tell itself when the time comes."

# CHAPTER FIVE

The Japanese man to the right of Jafet, the descendent of a feudal dynasty, cleared his throat and cupped one side of his face with his hand while leaning on the armrest of the chair. He smiled and narrowed his eyes as he looked around the circle of people. Then he lifted his wineglass and looked through it as if recalling the past.

"Many consider Japan to be the most haunted place in the world," he said. "Our beliefs revolve around the spirit world, so it shouldn't surprise anyone that we love to tell ghost stores. When I was a child in Japan, school was very difficult. I think you've heard of how hard elementary school can be. The discipline in some schools borders on child abuse. There's a saying—the nail that sticks out will get hammered down. Imagine being a non-conformist in a society like this. Yes, we are bright and exceptional in Japan. There is little crime and everything seems wonderful, but I'm sure you also know about our high suicide rate.

"Let me tell you about a friend I had in school. His name was Ushio. I felt a deep connection with him. Whenever I experienced something, I would wonder—how would Ushio handle this particular thing or what would his reaction be? For some reason, I felt that the both of us were rather artistic. I don't know why. It was just a feeling I had. But in our school—with the harsh discipline and intensive memorization—our minds couldn't drift off into imagination or daydream very much. It was almost as if we weren't allowed to be children. We were being toughened up, prepared for the world. Some teachers, I suppose, thought they were doing the kindest most compassionate thing in treating us like that. Just imagine how thick-skinned and impervious to life's difficulties we would be if we had harsh childhoods—or so must have been the thinking.

"Perhaps it was a good thing for some, but for many of us, the stress of going to school and experiencing these things everyday was more than we could bear. Some became very hostile towards others. The bigger kids would bully the weaker smaller ones in between classes. There was one bully that would come to pick on me, but sometimes he would pick on Ushio instead. It was a relief when he chose Ushio instead of me. Well, relief and guilt. I thought that we were so much alike that sometimes I would think that it was me that the bully was pushing around and hitting, when actually it was Ushio. And when it was my turn, I wondered if Ushio had similar thoughts.

"One day, the bully told Ushio that he was going to hurt him severely after school. It affected his demeanor that entire day. He dreaded the time that he would have to go home. I kept looking at him, knowing that it could just as easily have been me. In class, he would softly rock himself back and forth, breathing rapidly. His eyes were wide with apprehension. He couldn't have been able to think about it too much because of the memorization drills and the teacher's severe bearing. Questions were asked in the most punitive tone, frightening the child into full attention. But there was nothing to distract Ushio from the impending trouble—it was all there just underneath his outer awareness. Imagine such a fear and panic at a young age.

"And then I noticed him do something a child never does in class. He began to doodle. It startled me to see him do this. A stern scolding by the teacher was only moments away, I thought. And since I kept identifying with him, everything that happened to him, happened to me as well in an almost metaphysical way. He was sitting close to me, so I could see very clearly what he was doing. Quickly, and quite masterfully, he rendered a yūrei—the traditional ghost that begins to fade at the waist until it has no feet. It was the first time I had ever seen an artist draw anything. It was more than just a doodle. I marveled at it, and felt so inspired that I too wanted to develop artistic skills one day. As soon as he lifted his writing instrument from the paper, he turned the drawing over. The teacher never noticed a thing. I felt relieved for him.

"The next morning, my parents informed me that Ushio had committed suicide. They didn't tell me any of the details, so I wondered for days what had happened. I could picture the bully beating Ushio, and then Ushio going home and deciding that he had had enough of this world. And because I identified with him so much, there was a part of me that seemed dead. Perhaps it's better to say that my connection to a friend had been severed and now I felt strangely off balance—lonely. I don't know how else to put it. I felt this way—out of sorts as well as confused for a time. I had never known anyone who had died before. One moment they're here and then they're gone. And this wasn't just some person. It was me.

"I thought about the yūrei that Ushio had drawn and the possibility that he himself was planning on becoming a ghost. Did he think the bully would kill him, or had he prepared to take his own life? Imagine a little boy thinking about these things. I became fascinated with death, wondering what it was like to stop breathing and leave my body. I also thought of Ushio walking besides me. He became like an imaginary friend to me. I would talk to him in my thoughts, but sometimes I would notice my lips moving. I would quickly bite them so that no one would see me.

"Sometimes I would begin a drawing, but soon crumple it in frustration. I just didn't possess any of the magic that Ushio had. But then I could almost feel his empathy. I would talk to him and tell him how I wished to have artistic abilities. He seemed to tell me that creativity comes from the dark side—that one should be careful with such things. These weren't so much words as impressions. Eventually, I found the courage to apply myself more and practice drawing on a regular basis. I did see some improvement over time. But what was this creative darkness all about? I knew it had something to do with the spirit world.

"One day, I drew an image of a torii gate. It is an entrance into a sacred place, but to me it symbolized a door between myself and the spirit world. I imagined myself stepping through the gate and greeting Ushio. Just when I finished the drawing, I felt the presence of someone behind me. I turned around in my chair, but saw no one. I continued to feel this presence most of the day. It made me so nervous that I wanted to tell my parents. But I was afraid they would get mad at me and blame me for causing all these things to happen because of my obsession with the spirit world.

"I went to sleep at the usual time, but woke up in the middle of the night. I looked up and in the semidarkness saw a hand coming out of the wall. I was so frightened that I fell out of my bed. I stayed on the floor looking at the hand until I finally fell asleep again. The next morning, my mother woke me and asked me why I had been sleeping on the floor. I told her that I didn't know why. She sighed and helped me get ready for school. During the day, I felt a presence behind me several times. I was afraid that I would never get rid of that feeling, or worse, I might encounter the hand again at night. I thought that I was being followed all day. On my way home from school, I saw a Buddhist nun. I told her that something terrible was happening, but that I couldn't tell my parents.

"She sat with me on a park bench and listened as I told her what had happened. It felt so good to tell another person. The two of us looked at a small bridge over a pond and watched the clouds, leaves and blossom petals floating by. When I was done with my story, she explained to me that I was being haunted by my friend, but that he only had the strength to manifest one hand in the physical world. She wrote a sutra on a piece of paper and told me to put it in the hand if I saw it again. That same night, I awoke at a late hour and saw the hand reaching out to me through the wall. I took the paper containing the sutra and put it in the hand. The hand gently took the paper and receded back into the wall. That was the last I saw of what my friend, Ushio, could manifest in this world.

"Years later, I heard about what had become of the boy that had been a bully at school. He had stopped attending, and I simply assumed that he had finally been expelled for his behavior. The truth is that he had also been haunted by a hand. He told his parents that an angry ghost had been reaching out to grab him every time he had been near a wall. A large pale hand would swipe at him, sometimes barely missing—other times leaving deep scratches on his skin. Every day, the hand would extend a little more out of the wall, sometimes successfully clutching at his clothes and pulling him so hard against the wall that he would bruise. His parents wondered if the boy was losing his mind.

"One day they found a large hole in the wall in the boy's room. They pointed a flashlight into the dark void and saw a pool of blood on the floor. When the police investigated, they determined that the boy had been violently pulled through the wall and could not possibly have survived the trauma. Nevertheless, they searched for him for days. His body was never recovered. I think back to these events now and remember what it was like to be a child—to be more sensitive, to see more than what adults can see. I've tried to never lose this childlike quality.

"After the disappearance of the boy, I had mixed feelings about bullies. Whenever I saw someone being bullied, I would always come to their rescue, even if I had to use force. However, I would feel a strange sympathy towards the bully as well. I presumed that they would eventually grow out of this faze and deeply regret the pain they had caused others. Or perhaps an unseen world would follow them around, tormenting the tormenter for the rest of time. As for Ushio, I can still see him. I can see him right now. I can see everyone I've ever had a close bond with who has stepped into the world of the dead."

The Japanese man blew out the second candle. The room darkened another shade.

Emily's eyes were sparkling. She adjusted her shawl as if comfortable in bed and having a happy dream. A man with short white hair and a trimmed beard indicated that he would go next. He paused for a moment so the group would have more time to think about the tale of the Ushio and his bully. Then with a scratch of his facial scruff, he smiled and nodded his intention to speak.

"Since we have a guest," he said. "Let me start off by introducing myself. I'm Father Richard Osf. I'm a Franciscan friar, ordained to the priesthood a very long time ago. I don't want to tell you exactly how long-"

The group chuckled.

"I'm in good standing with my parish and with Rome—although if anyone knew about my ties to this group, there would be pandemonium. Life is so short and people get worked up about the littlest things. But what can you do? Anyway, are you ready for a ghost story?"

The group excitedly nodded. At least one emphatic yes was heard.

"As you probably know, I do a lot of weddings and funerals. I love weddings, but as you can imagine, funerals, not so much. In fact, I quite dread them. One day, someone that had attended one of my memorial services came to me and told me that he had caught a ghost on videotape—right in front of me, as I was delivering a eulogy. I was skeptical, but then he showed me the footage. There seemed to be a translucent man standing next to the coffin. He took a couple of steps, and then the camera panned to something else, the videographer apparently unaware that he had captured something extraordinary. I asked that this video not be shown to anyone. I didn't want a media circus, after all. I didn't want my life's work to be remembered for something like this. I'd be the guy who stood next to a stupid ghost. Some legacy I would leave. The person was very kind and said he would comply with my wishes. Most people, I'm sure, would be tempted to do the talk show circuit, showing the whole world an apparition caught on video, and making a lot of money in the process. So, I was relieved that all this would be kept a secret. However, things would soon get a lot stranger.

"Moments after the man had left; I received a call from a funeral home informing me of a family that had requested a Catholic vigil service. It was a last minute decision, so I wouldn't have time to talk to relatives in depth and gather my thoughts. The deceased deserved his life story to be told in a coherent, thoughtful manner, not in a haphazard way by someone that had never known them or their loved ones. But how could I refuse at such a time of heartbreak and loss? I decided I would try to learn as much as I could and take careful notes. Perhaps, I would be inspired to touch on universal themes that might be true for the young man that had died as well as his relatives. Maybe the reading of scripture would be a comfort to some.

"When I arrived at the wake, I was greeted by the man's parents. They told me that their son had finished school and had not been able to find a job. He had been considering going back to school and perhaps entering the priesthood. He deliberated enrolled at a theological seminary, but then realized that he wouldn't be able to afford the tuition. He became discouraged and would rant for hours about the hypocrisy of organized religion. His discouragement turned to hostility, writing anti-religious sentiments on his online blog, equating bible colleges and seminaries with prostitutes demanding money. One night, during dinner, he told his parents that he had been divinely called to serve as a priest—that he didn't know why those whores wanted so much money. Unable to sleep, he fixated on first and second year plans of study. Ancient Philosophy, Modern Philosophy, Humanities—The Greek World, Theology—Introduction to Scriptures I, Pastoral Ministry 101, Medieval

Philosophy, Contemporary Philosophy, The Roman World, Practicum, Ethics, Social Ethics, Fall, Spring, Summer, Winter—he taught these things to himself online, downloading and studying textbooks. Of course, he knew that none of this would ever result in a degree.

"His parents worried about his deteriorating mental health. They even grew afraid of him as he became more and more emotionally unbalanced. After many sleepless nights, he revealed his plan to commit identity theft and somehow impersonate a priest. He cursed this world for making it necessary to steal from another the very thing he felt he was called to do. If his plan failed, he reasoned, he would make it his life's mission to destroy the Christian church and rebuild it from scratch. His tirades would conclude with angry outbursts. 'All options are on the table! Priestly blood may have to be spilled! Death to the clergy!'

"Of course, this was a bit upsetting for me to hear. I quickly realized why the parents had been hesitant to seek out a priest for the wake. I asked them to recount fond memories of their son. They told me that he had always struggled with anger and self-control. The only thing that he had ever shown an interest in was the priesthood. I asked him why he hadn't gone to seminary, instead of a secular institution. The father admitted that he was to blame. He had always told his son that a real man makes money in a competitive career. Becoming a priest would be a lazy way to earn a living, mooching off the donations of others. He also revealed that he may have been too harsh in raising his son, beating him one too many times.

"I asked them again if they could recall any fond memories of their son that they could share with me. After a moment of silence, they conceded that they couldn't. There were times the mother had dressed him in clothes she thought were cute when he was a toddler, but for the most part, they couldn't remember anything pleasant about him. His life seemed to be marked by a nebulous discomfort that grew into resentment and eventually rage. The night his car drifted into the opposite lane and collided head-on with a semi, they had been considering calling the police because of his incessant rants about killing members of the clergy. When they told me this, I thought for a moment about the close proximity of our parish and the likelihood that I would have been the one sitting behind a desk in the only lit room in the church—and how easy it would have been for the young man to find me and take my life. I even wondered if he had been on his way to kill me the night of his accident. I felt a strange sense of relief that he wasn't in this world.

"So how could I speak at the wake? What would I say? There wasn't the tiniest thing about his life that seemed suitable for me to celebrate and share with his large family of aunts and uncles, cousins and distant cousins. Not only that, he may have been my failed assassin. My mind was filled with these selfish and, I admit, paranoid thoughts. But, I am human after all. So what I decided to do was simply do a reading from scripture and make vague and general comments about life and death and how we should all reflect on our own lives and our capacity for compassion. I know—it was rather hypocritical of me to say these things, when the truth was that I was glad this person wasn't around to hurt anyone.

"After I had finished speaking to the parents, I approached the casket. The corpse was that of the young man that had visited me earlier in the day to show me a video recording of a ghost. The shock hit me with a palpable blow that almost knocked the breath out of me. I put my hands on the side of the casket to steady myself. I felt my forehead tingling with perspiration as a chill entered my body. Trembling, I turned to walk away from the dead body and towards a microphoned podium where I was supposed to speak. I wiped my forehead with a handkerchief and turned to the Psalms. As I was about to read, my mind went into a fog. I was unable to speak. And then I saw the ghost of the young man by the casket, his attention on me. He lifted his hand to point at me. 'I died because you caused me to hate you,' he said.

"I looked in horror at his accusatory eyes. For a moment, I almost wanted to blurt out that I had nothing to do with seminary tuition costs. But, I had enough presence of mind to realize that there were many people in the room looking at me, expecting me to say something uplifting—not just uplifting, but perfect sentiments that would bring closure and justify this young man's existence. Perhaps, his disappointed parents had waited a lifetime to see if somehow a priestly perspective could make sense of their son's life. It was obvious that I was the only one that could see his ghost. All eyes were upon me.

"I cleared my throat and tried to form a word, but no sounds left my mouth. 'Are you all right, Father Osf?' asked one person. I nodded and proceeded to flip though the Psalms as if trying to find the precise verse to sum up all things. The fog in my mind thickened and I became confused. I panicked. I didn't know what to do. 'Why don't you let me help you?' said the ghost. 'I never received the ordination I wanted. I never experienced the glory and splendor of wearing a robe of righteousness. I never delivered a homily. However, if you preach the sermon I wish, I will go away and leave you alone.'

"These words produced terror in me. Was this some sort of celestial trial to test my faith? Would I agree to such a dark deal with a troubled soul? And then it occurred to me that I would go along with the apparition's wish, delivering a sermon from the world of the dead. The moment the ghost said anything objectionable, contrary to doctrine and good taste, I could simply close my mouth and leave. I would tell people that I wasn't feeling well.

"I agreed with a nod, and the ghost proceeded to orate his ecclesiastical discourse. 'Let there be an expanse in the midst of the waters, and let it separate the waters from the waters. This expanse will be called sky…' Obviously, he was quoting from the first chapter of Genesis. I had no idea where he was going with this. Was I falling into a trap to bring dishonor upon the priesthood? Would this be his revenge? I repeated the words and then the apparition continued. 'Why is it that God does not consider this day to be good as he does other days? The following day, God creates the lands and the seas, and says that they are good. But why not the day he created the sky? Why, pray tell, is the sky not good?'

"Now he had my curiosity. I have to admit, I wanted to know the reason. Why did God not say he that the day he created the sky was good? I slowly repeated the words to the mourning family. I could tell by the looks on their faces that they were perplexed at my choice of words for a remembrance service. This, after all, was to be a loving tribute to a man whose life was tragically cut short. I turned my head to gaze intently upon the phantom orator, expressing my inquisitiveness. The family were probably wondering why I was so distracted by the casket. Perhaps they assumed that I was overwhelmed by emotion. Little did they know what I was seeing and what was taking place. I widened my eyes to convey my eagerness in hearing the reason for why the sky was not good.

"The ghost stared at me with vacant smile. I waited, almost desperately for him to continue. But he just leered at me, like an ice-covered statue withholding the answer I was expecting. After about a minute, he disappeared. I took a deep breath and noticed that my heart was still racing, my face perspiring and my hands were still trembling. I looked back at the grieving family and threw together some general observations about coping with loss and read scripture. Although the ghost of the young man had vanished, I could still feel his presence. I left the wake as soon as I was finished, foregoing the comforting of family and friendly conversation.

"I went into the restroom and in the mirror I saw the apparition's reflection. I nearly fainted. I stormed out of the funeral home and kept seeing the image of the ghost reflected on window panes and in the puddles in the streets. The whole time I was driving back to the parish, I felt a slight tug on the steering wheel, as if the ghost wanted me to drive into oncoming traffic. I arrived back, practically in tears. I went to my room and put away anything that could produce a reflection. The following morning I awoke and could no longer feel the presence. I went on my computer and checked my emails. The first message I read was from a long time parishioner that would try to stump me with bible questions. She wanted to know why the sky was not good. To this day I don't know the answer."

Father Osf blew out the third candle and the room was almost dark.

# CHAPTER SIX

## A Month Before the Murder

Emily awoke as she did the previous morning, excited and almost unbelieving that she was in Kyoto. In the short time she had been at the hotel, the furniture had become cluttered with packages of Japanese snacks, coins, tourist leaflets, booklets and receipts, everything a souvenir. It was still quite early. Her body hadn't adjusted to the time difference yet. She clicked through the television channels. Most of it was a little too silly, even for her taste. The entertainment was often a comedy reality competition with an inset of a separate camera feed to show the viewer someone's reaction to the focal programming. The Japanese seemed to like having a little head always in the corner of the screen, smiling or looking shocked or surprised. She had to wonder if perhaps the Japanese didn't understand humor all that well. Could it have been that they simply equated comedy with being ridiculous? And what was this obsession with the little talking head cam?

She found a station that was broadcasting a children's program. It looked like something she had seen once at the Broward Center of the Performing Arts, a large auditorium with a beautifully lit stage. Vibrant purple curtains and bluish lights presented a pageant of fantastic creatures that looked like enormous puppets. The children in the auditorium sang along with an orchestra. Emily found the music to be so soothing that she closed her eyes and let the sounds tingle down her spine.

She went to inspect the bathroom again, amazed at how efficiently they had laid out the tiny room. The sink overlapped slightly into the shower, and everything seemed to be designed in an ingeniously space-saving manner. The toilet was an altogether different matter. Never had she seen anything so complicated with all its knobs and buttons labeled in kanji characters. She decided not to attempt anything more advanced than simply flushing.

In the mirror, she saw herself tired and disheveled but clearly radiating her excitement from being in Japan. She couldn't help but smile and talk to herself as she had done before, role playing for her ASMR videos which she liked to upload to YouTube.

"It looks like you take good care of your skin," she said softly. "When was the last time you were here for a facial? Oh, I see. I'm going to apply a little cleanser now. It's slightly abrasive."

Emily burst into laughter and then held her gaze for a moment. She went and got her phone, turning on her camera to the video setting and returning to the mirror. She held it up and selected the record button.

"Hi—sorry about the quality of this video, she spoke in a hushed tone. "I'm just using my cell phone. The sound is probably not good enough for ASMR, so I'm just gonna to tell you what I'm up to. I'm in Kyoto. I can't begin to tell you how happy this makes me. It's a lifelong dream of mine to come here. As you might know, I'm really into all things anime and manga. I've been crazy about this stuff since about fourth grade thanks to the Cartoon Network. But it's not just that, the entire culture fascinates me. You might say I'm a Japanophile. Geisha, Samurai, origami, bento boxes—you name it. I'm a big fan. Anyway, I'm gonna to try to enjoy everything as much as I can while I'm here. I'll do more role-play videos soon. Thank you to all my subscribers. You mean so much to me. I'll try to be here as much as I can. I just need to balance my life and make more time for you. But even now—here in Japan—I'm thinking about you. I'm glad you enjoyed my reading you a bedtime story. It's so nice to know that I talk and read so many of you to sleep—that I'm the last thing you hear and see at the end of your day. I love you so much. I just wanted you to know that I was thinking about you before I get going. I'm not sure if I'll be able to post this video until I get back from my trip. I might not have time to edit it, and I don't know if I'll have enough bandwidth to upload. But I just wanted to do this for you guys. Love you—bye."

Emily showered and went down the street about a block to a McDonald's. She chuckled at the thought of having breakfast at an American fast food restaurant while in a foreign country. After receiving her order, she climbed the stairs to the second level and sat by a large window to people watch and use her phone. She had been having trouble with the hotel Wi-Fi, but now could check her email. There were two new messages with subject headings that appeared to be related to her video channel. The first one simply said thank you for the tingles. She beamed as she scrolled through the compliments, and at the end, a request for a specific role play. Someone wanted her to be a nurse. The other message was a simple question from a curious fan. What are your favorite television programs? There were at least two videos that needed to be made. One in which she answered viewer questions, and most likely, another involving scrubs and a stethoscope.

Next, she opened her Kyoto Visitor's Guide app and tried to figure out her itinerary for the day. She could get to most of the places of interest from Central Kyoto on foot. The only place that seemed too far to walk to was the Golden Pavilion on the grounds of the Rokuon-ji temple complex. She had wanted to see this Zen Buddhist temple mainly because she had read the novel by Yukio Mishima with the eponymous title. However, the prospect of catching two different subway trains to get there caused her agitation. She found the directions on the guide app confusing and opened a second Visitor's Guide app. After struggling for a while, she took out a paper map from her pocket and carefully studied it.

Later that morning, she managed to find her way to the Golden Pavilion, successfully using the Japanese subway for the first time. The three story structure was said to be covered in gold leaf in order to purify negative attitudes towards death. For Emily, death had always been a fascinating world of spirits and tantalizing mysteries. Her only experience with loss had been the passing of a goldfish as a child. She had never known bereavement whether a friend or relative. She sometimes thought of herself as already in the spirit world. In Japan she could roam the streets like a ghost, admiring its beauty and not needing to bother anyone unless she had to order a meal.

How interesting it would be to haunt a city like Kyoto, she thought, free from all emotion and drama, problems and responsibilities. It would be like walking through a museum venerating great paintings, and never having to experience the artist's tortured life. Or like a camera crew that covers a sporting event, ecstatic over the up-close experience of watching talented athletes perform wondrous maneuvers in the physical world, apart, above and detached from the pain of injury or the trouncing by an opponent. Emily also knew there were advantages to being alive as well such as the singular opportunity to make a mark upon the world. Despite being misunderstood and all the distresses of living that have to be dealt with, something may be accomplished—the satisfaction of some elusive desire. No ghost can ever achieve such a mark.

Emily thought of her video channel as an artist's canvas, her little impression of the world to be remembered by. Of course, it might soon be forgotten, but it was her expression and possibly someone's heart-response that ultimately mattered. Despite her youthful preoccupation with Japanese animation and novel superficialities, she was an old soul. She was aware of many great and simple truths. She knew, for instance, that love is not something that people can easily understand. It comes with much time and experience. A young person may know infatuation, a young couple may know clinging, but the wise soul knows that mature love involves much more. For this reason, Emily understood the importance of not to making it a top priority to find a mate.

She did, however, fret a great deal over her older brother's love life. She huffed whenever she thought of a reality so plain that she could categorize it as fact and certainty. Her brother, Eliot, was even more sensitive than she was. My God, she would think. How was this possible? His eminent engagement to a petite and boisterous woman was like a ship about to hit an iceberg. What would happen to him after a year of marriage when he finally realizes that being in a relationship would not solve his problems? Would it even last a year? Her temper and selfishness would surely drive him to despair.

Emily desperately wanted to save her brother from this fate and somehow prove to him that it is much harder to die of loneliness than it is to die of heartbreak. One gets used to loneliness, but relationships have a brutal quality to them that no one can ever fully anticipate. Of course, most guys are insensitive enough to survive the rest of their lives being screamed at and despised by their wives, but her dear brother, Eliot, would internalize it all and most likely wind up hanging himself. It was a thought that came to her once and now she couldn't get that image out of her head. Someone such as Eliot was better suited composing his symphonies behind the keys of a piano than opening his heart up to pain.

A few disastrous short-term relationships might help him to write better music, but this god-awful matrimony with what Emily perceived to be the queen of darkness would be like the power surge that blows out Eliot's mind. Being the over protective younger sister, how could she keep from disliking his girlfriend? People needed to be protected from harm. That was Emily's underlying feeling about the world.

There were many others that Emily also worried about. But to concern herself with her own demise seemed ludicrous to her. Death was like a tantalizing riddle that intrigued her to no end. It wasn't something that she sought after, but neither was it anything that frightened her. Death could be thought of as a friend that constantly reminds a person to appreciate their worries and troubles, for they would surely all come to an end. But what if there was no end at all? What if an afterlife came with its own set of worries and troubles?

As Emily studied the gold leaf on the pavilion walls, she also considered a third possibility. It was a Zen Buddhist temple after all. Perhaps there was a middle ground and the answer was a bit more profound than simply yes or no. If everyone's life was an extension of the fabric of the universe, it was a joy simply existing, whether a creature or a tree. But what does one do when they are caged or planted in a tiny pot? The days were going quickly by and soon Emily would be back in her cubicle, staring at a computer screen for eight hours and talking to clients on the phone, no longer roaming the streets of Kyoto with her gleeful gaze.

How would an enlightened monk adapt to the practical world of earning a salary and stomaching the moods of those who took themselves too seriously? It would be easy to retreat to a place of silence and solitude. Isn't that cheating? She wondered. Supposedly, a spiritual master is unfazed by all things. But wouldn't it be easy to demonstrate inner peace if you don't have to deal with angry webcasting clients? Yes, the corporations are paying a fortune to stream their quarterly earnings events seamlessly, but that's no excuse for rudeness—and would a Zen master be able to maintain their tranquil composure? Would they truly overcome all emotion and be fully appreciative of the beauty of the cosmos at all times?

Emily decided to stop thinking about her job and to be grateful for her short time in Japan. Even in this, she knew that she had a long way to go before taming the mind with all its incessant judgments and negativity. She looked at the temple as a whole, like a yellow sapphire rounded at the bottom with its reflection in the pond. After breathing in the beauty one last time, she walked back out of the temple grounds past the memento stands and found her way to the bus stop. A short ride later and she would be at the train station. However, this wasn't how things would turn out. She got off at the wrong stop and spent the next few hours lost in northern Kyoto.

Her phone apps were no help as she walked herself into a gradual panic, wondering what she would do if it became dark. Although she felt safe walking the streets of Japan alone, she had to wonder if she would ever find her way back to the hotel if the sun went down on her. She came upon a large grocery store. It was the largest thing that resembled a supermarket that she had seen in the city. Most places that sold food were small like convenience stores. She had asked several people earlier for directions, but no one could speak English. In the larger store she found a two people that had studied English but were too shy to speak to her. However, they appeared determined to help her.

Emily pointed to the train station on the sightseeing guide, and a young female cashier drew a diagram for her. After a moment, Emily realized that the symbols with three bubble shapes were traffic lights. She was to make a left turn after the third light and then she would find the entrance to the subway. The cashier and a male coworker walked her outside and pointed the way to get her started. They both smiled and bowed deeply. At that moment, Emily felt as though she had made two friends, and was almost reluctant to leave them behind. It was this way with practically everyone she met. She could somehow feel lives converging and then being torn apart. A human being with childhood memories and future descendants and all the millions of things that happen to them, for one moment looking into the eyes of another who share similar experiences. This happens for just a flash in time and then they are separated by seven thousand miles. The distance from Kyoto to Fort Lauderdale is forever, except for one week in a lifetime.

She arrived at the street her hotel was on around dinner time. She passed it and walked a little further to a restaurant that served food on skewers. There was a sign in the front welcoming English speakers and accepting Master Card, so she considered it a personal invitation. As the hostess was taking her to the back of the small kebab eatery, she noticed a woman sitting at the bar making a quick glance at her and raising her eyebrows for a moment. Emily barely noticed it yet felt wounded. It was the first time in Kyoto that she hadn't had a pleasant experience with a Japanese person. It also reminded her how sensitive she was. Looking so different from everyone and standing out should have rubbed someone the wrong way by now. She was grateful that by in large she had been treated well, but this tiniest of incidents seemed to sting a bit more than it should have.

As she was waiting for her order of grilled chicken on skewers with warm sake, she scrolled through the day's photos on her phone. The selfie she took with the golden pavilion in the background was her favorite. She regretted not getting a picture of the two employees of the grocery store that helped her find her way to the train station. It would have made for a more human experience than merely having a collection of touristy images. She thought once again of being a ghost and spending a day with them, learning all about their routines and the things that make their lives unique. How fascinating it would be to get to know every person on the planet.

As Emily was trying to delete a fuzzy picture of the golden pavilion, the gallery app closed and several other apps opened by themselves. Her phone had been acting funny ever since she had Brian, one of the network administrators at work, configure it to work as a remote for a video camera. Not only did apps mysteriously open and close, the battery didn't seem to last as long. She thought about removing the remote app from her phone but was too exhausted. She would get to it eventually, or since it was almost time for to renew her contract, perhaps she could trade the phone in for the latest version.

Emily went back to her photo gallery again to delete blurry images and crop the sharp ones. She looked across to where the woman that had raised her eyebrows was seated, trying to imagine her world. Maybe she had a few close friends who frequented that bar together after work every day. It might just be an idiosyncratic ritual they perform every time a stranger invades their social space. She thought about this for a moment and made peace with what had a short time ago caused her needless emotional distress. At least the woman hadn't rolled her eyes at her, Emily concluded.

The steaming skewers arrived and Emily thanked the waitress. The sake was heated inside a ceramic flask and served with a tiny cup. She quickly took a sip before the fermented rice had a chance to cool. As shy as she was and as much as she preferred to be alone, she began to crave someone to talk to. This would be another drawback of being a ghost, she thought. Unless spirits are in the habit of flocking together, they would roam the earth in a perpetual state of solitude. What would she do if she were somehow caught between two worlds? No longer in this one, but also not at the destination that souls arrive at.

She looked around at the people seated in the restaurant and promised herself that she would make an effort to get to know more people. She didn't know enough Japanese for this to be possible in Kyoto, but she had the rest of her life to work on this—hopefully, a long, healthy and prosperous life. Every person would become a gateway into the human collective unconsciousness, or some sort of porthole into infinity. One person at a time—she would be fully present, sincere and faithful in believing that her soul was reaching every heart with every minor thought and sentiment. She could be like an anime character with super powers. All this would be possible if she lived long enough and finally got over her shyness. The fermented rice seemed to make these things possible, like a river that doesn't realize how close it is to becoming an ocean.

# CHAPTER SEVEN

## The Night of the Murder

Father Osf's ghost story, known as a *kaidan*, had brought smiles to the gathering. Emily felt a mixture of pleasure and apprehension. She had thoroughly enjoyed the tale of the bitter ghoul that couldn't afford to attend a theological seminary, but now it was her turn to speak and summon the courage to blow out the last candle. She glanced up at the playful kijimuna hiding in the trees of the mural and used it as a source of inspiration.

"Don't be nervous," Simeon Suslov smiled.

"I can do this," Emily laughed and pretended to exude confidence.

She took in an exaggerated breath, raised and dropped her shoulders.

"Are there any rules I need to follow?"

The group smiled and shook their heads.

"All right, but I've got to ask—I tell a story, blow out the last candle and then what happens?"

"Nothing," Federico Carlesimo Jafet said. "And everything."

"Let me see if I can explain this," said the woman seated next to Emily. "We are unlike the world. People are for the most part normal and up to mischief, highs and lows and all the comedy and tragedy of life. They haven't quite lost their minds yet. The average man or woman is completely immersed in whatever they've been programmed to believe. All the square pegs fit nicely into square holes and the round ones slide perfectly into the round ones. Things are either black or white. If you would show them incontrovertible evidence that this is not the case, they would find a way to use this data to further support their beliefs. Without the programming, they would forever be swinging wildly like a pendulum between crime and addiction on one side, to arrogance and self-righteousness on the other. Sometimes the two sides meet and you have religious violence or some manifestation of war. Other times the pendulum hangs in perfect balance and a person realizes they don't ever want to return to all the swinging—all the drama. This is a very difficult thing, to be the odd one—the misfit. It's natural for a type of existential anxiety to reveal itself as the individual loses interest in the madness of life. A person may even begin to think that they are crazy. But the truth is that they are very close to piercing a thin veil that separates them from happiness. We, in essence, take our seats and look up at the stage, pleased to enjoy the stories being played out. We are a little like spirits. And so to celebrate this, we tell each other kaidan, ghost stories. When you blow out the final candle, it is symbolic of leaving behind the world of the living and preparing ourselves to be entertained. We will laugh and cry and mock the silliness of the mortals who actually think that everything fits together like pegs in holes. The truth is that everything is paradox, reality is messy. There is only one thing that is absolutely true: there are no absolutes."

"You can't prove anything to anyone?" Emily asked. "Everything is either black or white in most people's minds?"

"That is what is known as sanity," Jafet sighed. "There is nothing more natural than to be intellectually or emotionally unbalanced. Suppose you have some basic assumptions about life. Where did these assumptions come from? Essentially, ideas, worldviews, doctrines, party platforms—all these things reproduce and spread like viruses. Most people simply accept what they are taught and how the world works and don't question the status quo. Others are radicals and nonconformist or conspiracy buffs who believe they can change the world, but they don't realize that anything they turn the world into will be just reflection of their unbalanced mind."

The Japanese man nodded emphatically before speaking. "The eastern mind isn't as hopeless in these things. It is Greek civilization, then Roman and eventually all things western that break from any nondual thinking one might find Zen, Advaita or Taoism. The western ego loves argument and conflict. In the east, we try to not to see the world as black and white, but there is plenty of ego, and therefore plenty of war. How did emperors take themselves so seriously and take such offense at things? The answer is always arrogance. It is the nature of man. So what are we to do? We go against nature, becoming like celestial entities—fascinated, amused and entertained by all the earthly tales unfolding before us."

"But nothing can be done now?" Emily asked.

"We're in the dark ages," Suslov said. "Or at least that's a good analogy. Imagine if you lived back in the time of the inquisition or some ghastly time in history like that. People are being tortured to elicit confessions from so-called heretics. Out in public or in dungeons, men and women—being mutilated in the name of God. Or consider the Chinese practice of linchi that existed for a thousand years. Death was slowly brought on by slicing the body to pieces. Obviously, we are more civilized now. We consider these practices to be contrary to everything that is humane. But imagine if you lived during these periods. In your brief lifetime you probably wouldn't see an end to all this madness. All you could hope for would be the day that human consciousness would evolve to a higher degree. And that's how it is now in a way. All change occurs gradually. You do what you can if an opportunity arises, but for the most part remain patient and simply accept that the world is still asleep."

"And one day the world will wake up?" Emily asked.

"If God permits it," Suslov smiled. "Suppose one day humanity reaches a higher level of consciousness. They'll be fascinated by all the stories of battles and love affairs, treachery and betrayal, kindness and goodwill. They'll look back to the time when the earth was bubbling with drama. But a few of us do it now. We even make up our own stories."

"So much to think about," Emily said softly.

"Are you ready to pierce the veil," asked Jafet.

"I am," Emily said.

"Just to be fair," Father Osf said. "I had nothing to do with the inquisition."

The group laughed and then became silent, everyone looking at Emily.

"This is the story I would like to tell you," Emily said. "What do the Japanese call the spirit of someone who's not really dead—but having more like an out of body experience?"

"An Ikiryō," the Japanese man smiled.

"Ikiryō—let me tell you about an Ikiryō," Emily leaned forward to tell her story. "I was recently in Kyoto. The day that I was leaving Japan, I was having a hard time at the ticket vending machine at the subway station. I needed to purchase the right tickets to get me to the Kansai airport. All the buttons on the machine were written in Japanese. There was a little bit of English, but it made no sense to me. I was afraid that I would miss my flight. And then I saw him, the most beautiful man I had ever seen, a tall Japanese man in a dark suit and tie. He had such gentle eyes and wanted to help me, but didn't speak much English. Most of the Japanese don't. But somehow he understood enough to help me get my tickets.

"I had a pocket full or coins. I didn't realize how much they were worth. I could have bought more souvenirs—maybe kokeshi dolls or something like that. Anyway, I gave him all my coins and he pushed the right green and yellow buttons and out came my tickets. And then he returned what was left of my coins—still a pretty big pile of them—affectionately—with both hands. I didn't want to go anywhere. I almost wanted to embrace him and not let go. But I waved goodbye. He waved back. I smiled and he smiled. And after I went through the turnstile and towards the train, I felt sick. What if I had just met the love of my life and now he was gone? What a terrible thought—that this was some fluke encounter with the one person in the world that I had some uncanny connection with, and now I would never see him again. I know, it sounds stupid, but this is what I was thinking.

"On board the plane, that sickening feeling only got worse. I kept thinking that we were meant to be together—that our encounter at the train station had been divinely fated. With our waving goodbye to each other, we had, in essence, wiped away our children and their descendants and thousands of future people. Yes, mass murder. I know it sounds crazy, but it was as if I could see this perfect fractal pattern, endlessly repeating in all its beautiful splendor, and then a hideous beast had come and bitten a huge chunk out of it. I looked into the gaping hole and saw my future, or rather lack thereof.

"Needless to say, this put me into a bad mood. I was tired of thinking about these things and decided to distract myself with the inflight movie. However, there was a heavyset man sitting directly in front of me who kept rubbing his right ear. He wasn't just rubbing it, but vigorously squeezing and shaking it with the fleshy part of his palm. He did this so hard that I heard these horrible sounds coming from his inner ear—weeg-weeg-weeg. Normally, I wouldn't let something like that bother me, but I found it to be nauseating. I couldn't understand how no one else seemed to mind, even as the sounds got louder—weeg-weeg-weeg-weeg!

"When I arrived in New York for my layover, I actually felt traumatized by the many hours of having to listen to those horrible ear sounds. I also felt sort of claustrophobic in America—trapped among the uncaring big city people and already missing the smiles and deep bows of the Japanese. Why was it so hard for me to learn foreign languages? Maybe I could've found work in Tokyo or something like that. With perfect Japanese words, I could've thrown myself at that man in the train station. I've never done anything like that, but the what ifs were driving me crazy.

"As I sat waiting for my next flight, I read a manga on my phone. And guess what it was about—tiny supernatural creatures that enter people through their ears. I was tempted to close the app, but curiosity got the better of me. I learned about these tiny luminous entities that enter into people when they fall asleep. Of course it's all make believe, but—I don't know—maybe it was the jetlag—but I really started to wonder if that guy had rubbed his ears so hard that it sent some of those creatures in my direction.

"Supposedly, these things attach themselves to your brain and eat your memories. However, your subconscious mind gets to decide which memories they eat first. Your conscious mind might even be able to get in on the action, helping to sort through old and recent recollections. My attention seemed fixated on the man that had helped me at the train station. I couldn't quite decide whether or not I wanted to forget about him. It would be a relief to just remove him from my mind forever, but there was a part of me that didn't want to let go of how strange it was to feel such an instant attachment to someone else. I had to wonder if he was a real person or somehow served to represent a mystery. Perhaps, he was even like a blueprint or some archetype of what I needed to find or become.

"When I arrived in Fort Lauderdale and went back to my normal life, I went into a funk of sorts. The more anxious and discouraged I became, the more my energy drained from me. I could hardly sleep and was a mess at work. Who knows what my coworkers must have thought of me. I was probably mumbling all kinds of nonsense—I was so sleep deprived—maybe even about the things eating my memories.

"One night, as I lay in bed sleeping, I had the strangest sense that my body was separating in two. My head began to tingle and then the rest of my body. The tingles turned into strong vibrations as my dream body lifted up above my sleeping body. I floated away from myself, turning around to see my glowing face resting on the pillow. I don't know why it was glowing—only that perhaps I had a new kind of vision that could see living things as light. I soon became concerned that I wouldn't be able to get back into my physical body, so I went back and awoke. I was fine, only I wondered if it had all been real. Had the creatures in my brain given me special abilities? Or were these just extremely realistic dreams of out of body experiences?

"The following night, I decided to try an experiment. I was lying in bed at the threshold between wakefulness and sleep when I felt the vibrations shaking my body. What I did next, I can only describe as swimming up and away from myself. This time I decided to walk instead of float around. I went right through the front door of my apartment and on a stroll around the block. I knelt down to feel the coarseness of the sidewalk pavement. I touched the leaves on low hanging tree branches. I watched the occasional car pass by in the middle of the night. Everything seemed real.

"As I reached the furthest point on my walk around the block, I wondered again if I had strayed too far. Would I be able to get back into my body? My apprehension was less than the first time. I believed that there was a good chance that I would successfully reenter my body. Soon, I noticed that there was a golden retriever walking alongside of me. I stopped and asked if he could see me and he wagged his tail. Don't follow me—you'll get lost, I told him. He seemed to understand and went away. I got home, safe and sound in my body once again.

"On the third night, I decided to take my experiment further. Could I go anywhere? I felt the tremors taking over my body as I lay on my bed. I chose a faraway place and then I chose a faraway person that I couldn't stop thinking about—the handsome man from the Kyoto train station. To my astonishment, I was instantly standing next to him. He was home alone sitting at a table. He held the side of his face with one hand and stared off into nowhere. I looked around and saw that it was a kitchen with cabinets and shelves. There were cookbooks, wine bottles and plenty of pots, pans and utensils. I wondered if he was a chef or thought of cooking as a serious hobby.

"I turned back to him and examined his face for a while. He looked sad. I wanted to do something to cheer him up. Obviously, I had no idea what could be wrong. I was like a ghost. He couldn't see me and I couldn't even pour him a glass of wine. I sat next to him and looked at him for a while. It was nice to see him again. I was almost content just to be at his side, but I knew this contentment couldn't last long. What good was all this if I couldn't even talk to him or know anything about him?

"And then a thought came to me. Why not go inside him and take a look around? It might be an invasion of privacy. Or maybe it wouldn't. I just intuitively knew that this was something that I could do. It would be as natural as breathing. And so I moved closer and closer until my dream body was inside his physical body. He felt so warm. I can't even describe how intimate and magnificent this felt. I'm not sure I ever wanted to leave. I just wanted to be with him forever. This poor guy. He had an ikiryō inside of him—hope I said it right. An ikiryō in love with him.

"Almost immediately, I was eavesdropping on his thoughts. I tried to resist, but I couldn't fight the temptation. Tapping into his mental activity produced something of an impression. It was a sort of nebulous feeling that required that I spend more time with him to understand the complete picture. What I could tell was that he had lost his family. I wasn't sure if it had been some kind of tragedy or whether his wife had simply left him. At that very moment, he was experiencing a childhood memory, climbing a tree. As he made it to a thick branch, I decided to sit next to him. I thought to myself how much I liked being with him. I liked being with him in his kitchen. I liked sitting on a tree with him. If only he knew I existed.

"Suddenly, I felt a violent push. It felt as if I had fallen off the tree branch. I was on the kitchen floor and no longer in his thoughts. I looked up and was startled by the sight of a pale Asian woman staring down at me.

"'He belongs to me,' she said angrily.

"'Who are you?' I asked.

"'I've made him my home. You have no right to enter him!' she screamed.

"She started to move towards me like she intended to do me harm. I was so frightened that I immediately willed myself back to my body on the other side of the world. I awoke trembling, my body covered in sweat. I couldn't sleep the rest of the night. I decided that I didn't like my night time out of body activities so much anymore and would abstain from them for good. I went online and entertained myself reading social newsfeeds for the rest of the night until it was time to get ready for work.

"I struggled to stay awake the next day. I had four cups of coffee and was popping vitamin B as if it were candy. I was dreading the possibility that at any moment an angry client would call and yell at me for some error made on their webcast. The department manager had already been giving me looks that entire week. I didn't need a major screw up. My job is so stressful. We do so many of the Fortune 500 events. Everything has to be perfect. And here I am, doing crazy stuff at night no one would ever believe.

"I survived the day—went home, immediately craving my firm mattress. It seemed that the very moment I put my head on the pillow, I was sound asleep. I woke up in the middle of the night, needing to use the bathroom. When I returned to bed, I felt the vibrations again. At this point, I couldn't tell if I was awake or not. Even though I no longer wanted to pursue leaving my body anymore, I felt myself floating away until I was upright and standing on the floor. From across the room, I could see my physical body sleeping. I observed it for a little while, trying to decide in my mind if there were any worthy goals that I could achieve in this strange state. I wondered if perhaps I had been right to completely give up these things. Being able to go anywhere I wished was exhilarating. My life would be rather boring without these super powers. I just needed to stay away from handsome men. Surely, there would always be jealous female ghosts.

"As I was watching myself sleep and thinking of these things, I was horrified to see someone enter the room. It was the woman from the previous day. She was gripping a large knife with both hands and walking slowly to my physical body.

"'No!' I screamed.

"She glanced my way and then turned her attention back to the body that she was apparently preparing to stab. I lunged and grabbed one her arms. I realized that although we were like phantoms, the knife was real. It was the only thing between us that had any actual weight.

She was much stronger than me. It took great power to lift that knife—for her to manifest herself in the world in such a way. Clearly, she had been at this for much longer than I had, either as a ghost or someone that could travel in their sleep.

"We struggled and both fell on the floor, rolling on top of each other several times. Then she was over me. I couldn't hold back her arms any longer. She stabbed me in the chest and then the abdomen. I felt terrible pain as she slashed away. But there was no blood. There was no death. I could see that the woman was frustrated. She turned to look at my body asleep on the bed.

"'Please leave my sleeping body alone!' I pleaded. 'I won't go near him anymore!'

"As she was crawling to my physical self on the bed, I clung to her. She swung her arm back at me, stabbing me several more times. I thought I was being sliced to pieces as she dragged me behind her. I realized that I wouldn't have the strength to stop her. I screamed and pleaded, but she was determined to kill me. And then I threatened her.

"'If you kill me I will haunt him until the end of the world!' I howled.

"She turned to look at me. Her dark eyes penetrated my soul, searched it and found that what I had to say was true. She stared at me for a while longer and then dropped the knife. There was a slight leer in her expression as she delighted in the thought of having the man in Kyoto all to herself.

"'You will find someone just like him,' she said.

"And then she vanished. I awoke the next morning. On the floor by the bed was the chef's knife, the largest blade I owned."

Emily smiled and looked around at the group. Everyone smiled back at her. She blew out the last candle. The room went dark.

In the blackness a warm sensation blanketed the group. With eyelids closed, Emily felt herself almost in a dream where celestial entities could dance around her, ecstatic over the birth of fantasy into the physical plane. The discovery of symbols and clues had lifted a weight from her. These mysteries floated above, dispersing pain, doubt and insecurity. She couldn't remember the last time that she had felt confident. And now with a simple telling of a story, the darkness of the soul had been chased away. In the blackest darkness, she could see.

# CHAPTER EIGHT

## The Day After the Murder

Detective Ryan Salter stared at the crumbs on his plate. He had finished his medianoche quite some time ago and was pondering Simeon Suslov's account of Emily and her meeting with The Hermetic Order of the Mystic Koyosha. Detective Kim Ramos was staring blankly at the people going by on bicycles on Washington Avenue.

"And what happened after Emily blew out the last candle?" Salter asked.

Suslov shrugged. "It was dark for a short time and then someone turned on a few lights. We all started talking with one another. I got a little tipsy. That's all I remember."

Salter crinkled his forehead. "You don't remember anything that happened as you were drinking and becoming intoxicated? What was Emily doing?"

"It seems Emily was getting on well with the others. I think I saw her speaking with Jafet. I retired for the night inside the mansion. I was with someone, in case you're wondering about my alibi."

"Who were you with?" Ramos asked.

"Veronica, the woman who showed Emily the way to the

gathering."

"Do you know any reason why Jafet would want to harm Emily?" Salter asked.

"No. Jafet is the noblest of people. To insinuate that anyone in our gathering was capable of hurting Emily or doing anything criminal is offensive and ridiculous."

Ramos tilted her head and leaned into Suslov. "Emily Patrick attended your gathering last night and was found dead this morning. Something went horribly wrong. Did your group do anything besides tell ghost stories? Where there any other initiations or dangerous activities that you have failed to mention?"

"No," Suslov said.

"And all you have to say was that you were drunk and can't remember anything," Salter said.

"If I had known that I needed to give a detailed account of the evening, I would have paid more attention," Suslov said. "But, the truth is I was distracted by Veronica. I knew where things would probably be leading that evening. You can't fault me for failing to notice the rest of the room and everything that was going on."

"What's Veronica's last name?" Ramos asked.

"Jackson—Veronica Jackson."

"Can I have her phone number?"

Suslov reached in his pocket and pulled out his smart phone. He turned it on and scrolled through his contacts. After selecting Veronica Jackson, he turned the phone around to show Ramos. Ramos entered the phone numbers in her phone, stood up and walked outside the restaurant.

"She's going to call her now?" Suslov asked.

"Just a quick check of your alibi," Salter said and then looked at Suslov in silence for a while.

"That was an interesting talk you gave at Art Basel today," Salter said.

"Do you like art?" Suslov asked.

"I'm not sure I understand modern art," Salter said. "It seems to me that I can do modern art. I could make little piles of bricks and tie wires around them. Maybe I could paint one of the bricks white. Does that mean that I could sell my work for thousands of dollars? Oh, sorry—I forgot. I would also have to come up with a very elaborate and intellectual explanation for it. Isn't that right?"

Suslov closed his eyes for a moment. Then he looked at Salter with a soft smile. "The bricks and wire would be good. I think that would be good art. But remember, most of the high priced art you see never sells. Think of it as a fashion show. The models walk down the runway dressed in outrageous costumes. They look like creatures form alien worlds. No one would ever actually purchase clothing like that. It's just part of the big celebration of creative madness. It's all large and glamorous, but the truth is that most professional artists, the ones who sell their work for thousands, are desperate to sell just a few pieces a year so they can survive."

"But you're doing well," Salter said.

"Yes, I'm one of the extremely fortunate ones. Some artists are lucky enough to make a name for themselves. It's like when you buy an Armani suit. You may not know much about menswear, but you would be impressed if someone told you that they were wearing a designer name."

"At your talk, you made some disparaging remarks about the art world. Have you been having any sort of existential crisis?"

Suslov rolled his eyes. "All that is way in the past."

"Is there anything that you're very unhappy about now?"

"I'm at peace."

"That's quite a thing to say," Salter smiled. "How many people can say *that?*"

"It takes a long time to realize simple things."

"I bet," Salter said. "Your friend—Jafet—has he also realized some simple thing? Or could you be trying to see the best in him and overlooking something dark—something that doesn't quite make sense."

"He's the salt of the earth," Suslov said.

"There were around twenty people at your gathering. It's hard to imagine twenty people living perfect lives without any problems whatsoever."

Suslov made a faint sigh. "It's a group of very special people."

"Why did you invite Emily to join? Isn't it true that she hadn't yet achieved the peace that so permeated your group?"

"I could tell she was on the verge of having a breakthrough."

"How could you possibly tell that?"

"I just knew."

Salter looked at Suslov for a while. Ramos came back inside the restaurant and sat down.

"Checks out," she said. "Nothing about her tone or demeanor was out of the ordinary. You're quite the Romeo."

Suslov bit his lip and took a deep breath. "If only I hadn't abandoned Emily. I should've stayed with her and made sure she got home safe. I know it wouldn't seem appropriate to do that—to follow her home—but I feel as though there must have been something I could have done differently. At least I could have stayed sober so I could recount to you everything that happened at the gathering. I don't believe anyone in our group would have hurt her, but at least it would be better than just telling you that I couldn't remember anything."

"Are you concerned about this secret society of yours not being so secret anymore?" Ramos asked.

"Please try to be discreet with your investigation," Suslov said.

"Hopefully, we can close this case quickly and it won't turn into a big media circus," Salter said.

Ramos heard a buzz and glanced at her phone.

"Text?" Salter asked.

"Rob says that he and Hector will notify the victim's parents in a couple of hours."

"My God," Suslov sighed. "This is terrible."

Salter and Ramos continued to question Simeon Suslov for a while. Then they dropped him off at the convention center and headed to the Jafet mansion.

"Isn't taking a person of interest out to lunch against department policy?" Ramos asked.

"One can conquer the world with a little kindness…"

…

In the early evening, Salter and Ramos arrived at the home of Federico Carlesimo Jafet. They explained the nature of their visit and were invited to sit in his lavish living room filled with minimalist furniture. Jafet, in shock, couldn't close his mouth. He dug his fingers into his gray hair, massaging his scalp, the color from his face perceptibly draining by the minute. He stood for a moment, paced and then poured himself a drink and pressed something on the screen of his phone.

"Can I get you two anything?" Jafet asked.

"No thank you," Salter said.

Ramos shook her head.

Jafet sat down. "You spoke to Simeon already?"

"Yes," Salter said. "We went and heard him speak at Art Basel. Very interesting man."

"Indeed," he said.

"And how can I help you?" Jafet asked.

Ramos scanned a text message and looked up at Jafet. "Mr. Suslov got a little tipsy—as he put it—and then came inside this house where he spent the evening with Veronica Jackson. So he doesn't know what transpired at the—what do I call it—the chapel?"

"You can call it that," Jafet said.

"We'd like to know more about what happened at the chapel building in the back."

"Well—I couldn't wait to meet Emily," Jafet said. "I was impressed by her story. I'm not sure if she was familiar with the genre, but it was a classic Japanese ghost story she told. Well, as far as I'm concerned. I'm just an occidental that loves that sort of thing. We're all a bit fanatical when it comes to Japan. She had recently returned from a visit there. I was glad that Simeon had invited her to our gathering. She was the youngest person there, so it was like a breath of fresh air. I could sense that Emily had just become a new person—as if she had found a home, a family. Emily had told the story in such a way that it had cathartic effect upon her. I witnessed this. Her eyes—her mood—her energy all changed. After she blew out the candle, I knew that she was probably wearing a big grin in the dark. But I had to wait to speak to her. After the story she was like a rock star. She got mobbed—everyone wanted to introduce themselves to her.

"It was fascinating to watch a shy person glowing with confidence. Most people don't realize how important a part confidence plays in their lives. Especially, shy people. Shy people often attempt to be perfect and hope that no one ever notices them, but once they are on display, they try to be absolutely perfect for just a little while. Subconsciously, they fear rejection. A social situation is just a painful anxiety attack waiting to happen. But last night, Emily was a goddess. Her eyes were sparkling. She never stumbled over her words or missed a beat or hesitated or had an awkward moment. What a beautiful thing to see.

"As I watched her and her social magnificence I got the urge to play matchmaker. In her story, she described a Japanese man that she had briefly met at a train station in Kyoto. Our friend, Toshi, was like the elephant in the room. I wouldn't be surprised if everyone was thinking the same thing I was. Toshi Yamamoto actually has some ancient royal Japanese blood—a perfect prince for our Emily.

"I remembered the things she had said in her ghost story—that the Japanese man in the train station might have been some kind of representation—like a blueprint or some mystery to be solved. And then the jealous ghost at the end of the story tells Emily that she would find someone like him, and that now she knew the exact kind of man she wanted. It seemed like something so simple that one needed to explore the possibilities just so we could rule out the obvious and all get on with our lives."

"So you introduced Toshi to Emily," Salter said.

"Toshi had already said hi to her along with everyone else right after she had told her story, but I grabbed hold of him and brought him around for a second introduction. I left them alone and they seemed to like each other. Then they both went outside for a stroll, I guess. We have the lake with a dock. I doubt they used the jet ski, but the pier is perfect for star gazing. It was a perfect night."

"And that was the last anyone saw of Emily—leaving with Toshi?" Ramos asked.

"Yes, but Toshi didn't do anything to harm her. He would never hurt anyone."

Door chimes rang.

"Oh, he's here," Jafet said.

"Expecting company?" Salter asked.

"Yes, I'm afraid I pressed the panic button on the phone earlier."

"Panic button?" Ramos wrinkled her forehead.

"Yes—this is the worst day of my life. I called my priest."

Jafet opened the door and greeted Father Richard Osf with a two-handed shake.

Osf walked into the house. "What happened?"

"Emily is dead," Jafet said.

"Emily? Emily from last night?"

"Yes."

"What happened?"

Jafet walked Osf to the living room. Salter and Ramos stood to greet him.

"I'm Sergeant Ryan Salter. This is detective Kim Ramos. Maybe you can also help us in our investigation."

"Anything," Osf said. "What happened to Emily?"

"Emily was found dead early this morning," Ramos said. "She was at your gathering last night and we'd like to find out as much we can about what might have led up to her death."

"How did she die?" Osf asked.

"We don't believe it was an accident. We suspect foul play," Salter said. "Please help us. If there is anything you can think of that might help us figure out what happened we'd love to hear about it."

"I can't think of anything—I'm sorry to say. You might say she was the star of the party last night. We were all so happy to be around her—feeding off her excitement."

"But you saw her leave with Toshi Yamamoto?" Ramos asked.

"I saw her speaking to him. I didn't actually see them leave, but one moment they were there and the next both were gone."

"I'm sick. I'm absolutely sick," Jafet said.

"So am I," Osf said.

Salter narrowed his eyes with curiosity. "Just so I understand—I've heard a lot of talk today about how the group is enlightened and you guys have achieved some sort of inner peace. But I notice that you're both distraught with emotion right now. You wouldn't care to elaborate? Sorry—I just feel that I need to ask—not that it has anything to do with this investigation."

Father Osf sighed. "Well, I suppose if you're Saint John of the Cross or one of the desert fathers or a Zen monk, nothing would be able to faze you. We consider ourselves people that have had a genuine awakening. We're no longer fooled by the superficialities and emotional illusions and the mind games of the world, but when something like this happens—like what happened to Emily—all that nirvana stuff goes out the window."

"Glad to hear that you're human," Salter said.

"More human than you'll ever know," Jafet said.

"What can you tell me about Toshi Yamamoto?" Salter asked.

"Very special man," Jafet said. "His father was the head of a certain clan. I believe it had to do with a noble family in Japan. Toshi is a wealthy man—serves as honorary chair at a children's charity and does work around the world with the disadvantaged and those with special needs, especially in developing nations. He owns a home on a small island near the Venetian Causeway in South Beach. I've known him for about four years. He's as nice as they come."

"He never struck you as the arrogant rich kid type?" Ramos asked.

"Absolutely not," Father Osf said.

"No—no," Jafet said. "Not the least bit of pretention—completely faultless in character."

"How old is he?" Ramos asked.

"I believe he's twenty seven—thereabouts," Jafet said.

"What kind of car did he drive last night?"

"A new silver Lexus. I don't know what model."

"Do you know anything about his past relationships?," Ramos asked. "He must have had a lot of women chasing him around—after his money."

"He was very private. He didn't talk too much about it. I just remember him saying that he broke up with a girl in Japan a few years back."

"And here in South Florida—he didn't have women obsessing over him?"

"I wouldn't know anything about that," Jafet brooded.

"You really didn't know him that well," Salter said.

"We knew him well enough to know that he was a decent and honorable person," Father Osf said.

Salter chewed on his lip for a moment. "But you never know a person's hidden life. You don't know what kind of things he was mixed up in—what kind of vices."

"You don't understand," Jafet widened his eyes. "He's one of us. He just wouldn't hurt anyone."

"But like you said before, you're all human," Salter said. "Anything could have happened last night."

"I can assure you—Toshi is unlike anyone you've ever met. It's impossible to me that he would do anything to hurt Emily."

"Thanks for taking the time to talk to us," Salter said. "We just need Toshi Yamamoto's contact information…"

A few minutes later, Salter and Ramos were sitting in the car in front of the Jafet mansion.

"Not your everyday case," Salter said.

"Definitely not," Ramos said.

Salter rubbed his tired eyes. "At least it's a break from the juvenile violence. I needed this. I know it's morbid, but this is my one hundred fiftieth homicide. So often it's about teens defending their territory. Within a couple of years they go from children playing and getting along in school to teens shooting at each other. One group of kids live on Fourth Avenue and another group lives on Fifth, and because of that it's like trench warfare out there. I'm getting tired of it—tired of all the corpses piling up and all the inconsolable mothers. Weird rich people or the constant heartbreak that comes out of poverty—hmm—talking to weird rich people is a nice break for me."

"We should probably do an all-nighter," Ramos said. "It's getting late and we haven't spoken to what looks like the prime suspect yet."

Salter rolled his head on his shoulders. "I'll do an all-nighter. You should get a couple of hours sleep—say hi to your husband."

"I really want to meet this Toshi Yamamoto," she said.

"Okay…anything yet? What's taking them so long?"

Ramos scrolled through her text messages. "Rob and Hector are still going over the evidence. No sexual assault…no DNA evidence—cause of death—strangulation. They also found blunt force trauma to the back of the head. There was nothing useful in the foo dog drawings."

"So the perp was not interested in her sexually," Salter said. "And there's no struggle it seems. No perp skin under her fingernails. The drawings were scattered around her. I wonder if it was some sort of artistic statement, or the perp was offended at the lion-dogs. The way he laid her body out naked—it was almost as if the perp admired her—as if to say, look what I did to this beautiful thing."

"If it was Yamamoto, I wonder if somehow the lion-dogs were culturally offensive to him."

"Offensive enough to kill? We've already had several people vouch for his character. To be honest, the murder seems like classic nut job killing."

"And why would she let the perp kill him without a fight? According to everyone, she just had a peak experience. She must have been on such a high after her ghost story was so well received. She wouldn't have been depressed and welcoming death."

Salter shrugged. "The perp probably whacked her on the back of the head when she wasn't looking. But maybe she did have a major emotional crash. When you're on a high like that, it hurts coming down."

"Maybe Yamamoto got her hopes up and then crushed her heart."

"Or someone that wanted Yamamoto to herself."

"A jealous woman—you're thinking of the ghost story," Ramos smiled.

"How strange would it be if she actually knew she was in danger—if she left behind a clue for everyone?"

Ramos' phone buzzed. She read another text message.

"It seems Emily was a big deal on YouTube," she said.

"Really?"

"She had an ASMR channel—over seventy-five thousand subscribers."

"God—it takes a whole day to find out something that seventy-five thousand people could have told us."

Salter and Ramos drove to the guardhouse at the entrance to the community. They examined security camera footage from the previous night and then set off to South Beach.

# CHAPTER NINE

It was dark when Salter and Ramos arrived at the Yamamoto home. The sergeant turned off the engine and tapped the steering wheel a few times, admiring the two story Mediterranean style villa.

"I really don't feel like hauling this guy up to Broward County for questioning," Salter said. "We'll probably know if he's lying. It's just a matter of whether he looks right or left. If he lies, we'll take him to the station and conduct a formal interrogation a little empty room with three chairs. I'll lay down my version of the Reid technique—that'll be fun. But maybe it won't come to that."

"How would you interrogate someone like that?" Ramos asked.

"What do you mean?"

"Normally someone pretends to be like the suspect. The more you have in common, the more the person opens up. But what about someone that's from a totally different world. You and I can't even imagine what it's like to be Toshi—to be ultra-wealthy—to be Japanese. Japan is like another planet. They think completely differently from the way we think."

"I keep forgetting you've been there," Salter said.

"Being in Japan—you can't really get into people's heads. All this stuff is what I read later. Then you say things to yourself like, no wonder the man wouldn't give a straight answer and seemed so evasive. They don't like to say no."

"That's a good point," said Salter. "So if Yamamoto seems strange and suspicious, it could just be cultural stuff."

"Exactly."

"But what if he's really different? What if looking to the left means he's telling the truth? What if Japan is so opposite of us that everything is in reverse? You know, like toilets flushing clockwise in the southern hemisphere-"

"That's the most ridiculous thing I've ever heard," Ramos laughed. "Besides the flushing thing is a myth."

"It is?"

"Yeah, and all this talk about how different the Japanese are—is bordering on racism. We're all human."

"You're right."

"So we'll just be sensitive to cultural issues and leave it at that."

"We do the best we can."

Salter and Ramos got out of the car and approached the house. Toshi Yamamoto heard the doorbell and came to the door, greeting the two. He invited them in and soon the detectives were questioning him. When Toshi learned about Emily, his heart sank.

"Would you mind if we went outside?" Toshi said. "I need some fresh air."

"Not at all," Salter said.

The three went in the back yard where there was a swimming pool and garden overlooking Biscayne Bay and the lights of the Miami skyline.

"What a gorgeous view," Ramos said.

"Thank you," Toshi whispered.

They all sat down by the pool. Toshi cupped his hands up to his face.

"She's dead?" Toshi asked.

"I'm afraid so," Salter said.

"She's dead," he whispered out into the bay.

"I'm sorry to bring you such bad news," Salter said. "Please understand that we need to conduct a thorough investigation. Since you were one of the last people to see her alive, we were hoping you would tell us everything you remember about last night. We saw surveillance video from Jafet's community cameras and know that the two of you left in separate cars. Did you go straight home?"

"Yes, I came straight here."

"You guys left very late. You must have talked for quite a while."

"We did."

"What was her mood like the last time you saw her?"

Toshi smiled sadly. "I think she felt what I felt."

Ramos lifted her head and narrowed her eyes.

Toshi heaved a sigh and turned to stare out at the bay. "I wonder if she felt what I felt. I don't know how else to put it—love. Love is what I felt."

"So you had a romantic evening with Emily," Salter said.

"We talked and talked and bonded and everything was perfect," Toshi said. "I thought I was walking on air this morning. I thought about last night and I couldn't stop smiling. We promised we would call each other this week and go on an official date next Saturday. I wanted to call her today, but I didn't want to scare her off."

"You don't mind if we use your Sun Pass information to confirm that you drove straight home?"

"No, I don't mind."

"Did she say anything that may have sounded like she had enemies or was in any kind of trouble or danger?"

"No—I can't remember her saying anything like that."

"Can you think of any reason why anyone would want to hurt her?"

"No—unless they were jealous of such a perfect person."

Salter tilted his head with interest. "You thought she was perfect?"

"To me she was. Her temperament was the perfect mixture of so many things. As you can imagine, when you have money, people act differently around you. Even in Japan, things are complicated. I don't like the upper class women of Japan so much. They can be quite extreme when it comes to matters of finances, particularly matters of revenge. I have a fondness for the middle class but it's hard bridging the two worlds. I don't know if you understand. But Emily was so exotic to me—so different and with an intuitive wisdom about the world that she seemed like a library to me that I could spend the rest of my life reading."

"Are things really that different for you because you're upper class Japanese?" Ramos asked.

"It's certainly true that descendants of Samurais and the feudal ruling class do much better than the general population. I'm expected to marry someone from the upper echelons of society—someone like me. Being on the other side of the world—here in Florida—I have more freedom to explore and find what suits me best."

"Someone like Emily?" Ramos asked.

"I thought I had found my soul mate last night. And now—I have nothing."

Salter tensed his brow. "You said something about rich Japanese women with extreme jealously. Anyone like that in South Florida right now—someone that could have hurt Emily?"

"No. No one like that."

"Have you ever been stalked by anyone?"

"No."

"Could a wealthy woman from Japan have hired someone to follow you around and eliminate any romantic competition?"

"I doubt that," Toshi shrugged.

"How did you become involved with the Mystic Koyosha?" Ramos asked.

"Over time you meet people at fundraising events. I've donated quite a bit of money to the Morikami Museum over the years. It was inevitable that I would gravitate to people who had similar interests as I do. You talk to someone and discover that they think as you do. You dig further and find they share all of your discernments and insights and then you dig some more until you find that they are exactly like you."

Salter glanced at the city skyline and back at Toshi. "That must be rare indeed to find westerners who think as you do."

"Yes, the Japanese mind is a bit different. But with perennial philosophy, there are universal truths."

"Interesting," Salter said thoughtfully. "I could spend a lot of time with the Mystic Koyosha listening and learning."

"Can I ask you something?" Toshi took in a deep breath and slowly let it out.

"Yes, of course."

"How do you cope with so much tragedy on a daily basis?"

"It's our job," Salter said. "We get used to it."

Ramos clutched at her arms, trying to warm herself. "You don't have much crime in Japan-"

"Not that much, but just the other day I was reading in The Asahi Shimbun about a little boy who was stabbed to death many times. DNA matched the knife of the suspect. So right now, there could be someone like you in Japan doing the very same thing as you. So, no, I don't think America is the land of savages."

"I'm glad you don't think that," Salter said with a note detachment.

Toshi noticed Ramos trying to warm herself.

"I'm sorry. Are you cold?"

"A little."

"Let's go inside. I like Florida this time of year, but it does get a little chilly by the water."

The three went inside and sat on stools by the island in the kitchen.

"Did you touch Emily at all—kiss her goodnight?" Ramos asked.

Toshi raised his eyebrows and softly sighed. "We slow danced."

"Hmm. Did you know that Emily was famous?"

"Famous? No," Toshi clenched his brow.

"She had many thousands of subscribers on her YouTube channel. Do you know what ASMR is?"

"My niece does that," Toshi said. "It's very popular."

"It's videos of people giving each other the tingles, right?" Salter said.

"It's a lot more than that," Ramos said.

"Well, I suppose some people can have intense reactions to it."

"Very intense," Ramos said.

"Maybe Emily didn't mention her YouTube channel because she didn't want you to think she was strange."

"We talked about so many things," Toshi said. "It just didn't come up. I'm sure she would have told me eventually."

Salter put his hands together and exhaled. "I don't think you did this, Mr. Yamamoto. But you were the last person seen with her. There must be something that happened or was said that you're not remembering now. Can you please go over the events of last night? We know that Mr. Jafet introduced you to her. What happened after that?"

"I had shaken her hand before and told her my name," Toshi said. "Right after she had told us the yūrei—the ghost story. When Federico introduced me to her, we held hands just a tiny bit longer. Her smile—her eyes told me that she was glad we were together again."

"I'm sorry to interrupt," Ramos said. "Back to the ghost story—as you know—she meets man in a Kyoto train station. While she's sleeping, her spirit or astral body or whatever you call it visits the man at his home in Japan. Then, a jealous apparition tries to kill Emily, but then tells her that at least now she knows the type of man she wants. Was Emily looking at you the whole time she was telling this story? Do you think the whole thing was intended for your ears? Could she have known something about your wealth? Could she have been working for someone trying to find out information about you who then had her killed when she had accomplished her goal?"

Salter groaned softly, his eyes mocking her.

"What?" Ramos said. "Shouldn't we ask these questions?"

Salter lifted his open hands to indicate that he would give Ramos license to ask whatever questions she wanted.

"No," Toshi said. "She wasn't looking at me while she was telling the yūrei. There was nothing premeditated. Emily was not a con artist. Fate brought us together."

"I hope I haven't said anything offensive," said Ramos. "I'm a rookie detective, please excuse me."

"No need to apologize."

"Okay," said Salter. "You and Emily were shaking hands for the second time. What happened after that?"

"I told her her yūrei story was excellent. She told me that coming from me it was a great compliment. I said to her that I was sorry that she had such a hard time finding people in Kyoto that spoke English. I asked her if it had been her first time to Japan and she said yes. She told me that she had only stayed a week and was sad to leave. And then I told her that I thought I could guess which parts of her story were true and which were fantasy, but I promised her that I would not ask. Then I congratulated her for her samurai courage and blowing out the last candle. I told her that I was very happy that she was part of the Mystic Koyosha.

"We said a lot of things to each other. I can't remember all the things we said, but we made each other laugh quite a bit. I felt witty around her. Everything I thought to say was on target. I couldn't remember the last time I was so happy to be around someone. Her brown eyes were sparkling. You should have seen her beautiful eyes. I had this feeling that she had broken through to a new stage in life and that I could help her understand so much more. I had the key to many confidences and I wanted to give it to her as a gift. Sometimes when a person is crushed by life events, when they feel like they've hit the bottom, it's actually the start of something new and wonderful. Emily was depressed after she got back from Japan. It was for a short time, but it was a deep despair. Somehow, she had the strength to search for answers. Little did she know her email to Simeon Suslov would lead her to the Koyosha and then eventually to me.

"I wanted to be her friend, her teacher and someone to love. She captivated me—filled me with a longing to be these things. I kept glancing at her eyes and lips and the beautiful color of her skin, and said to myself, I must share my knowledge with her. Not just because of her stunning appearance, but because she radiated an inner light. This fire inside her, it needed to be fed. I needed to throw more onto the flames. I knew she was special—receptive to ancient wisdom—things that are as plain as day, but few ever understand. There are very few in this world that that possess true wisdom."

"You understand true wisdom?" Ramos asked.

"I don't understand why she died. I don't understand how to cope with her loss. I don't understand many things, but I happen to know a few essential things about life. And there are many things I would like to know. I thought we would have a long time to explore all the mysteries together."

"Things don't always turn out the way we want them," Ramos said.

"Maybe she didn't need me. Maybe she was ready for a new life or new world."

# CHAPTER TEN

## The Night of the Murder

Toshi and Emily sat on the pier by the lake, both holding their phones up to the sky. They read the names of constellations off of the planetarium app. Jupiter, Mars and Saturn were all present that night, Roman gods conferring and conspiring. The belt of Orion shone brightly in the cloudless atmosphere. Emily made side glances at Toshi. Toshi kept noticing that whenever he looked at Emily, her star lit face would steal his breath away.

"Orion is like the long sleeve of a kimono," Toshi said. "Imagine a woman extending her arm out."

"A woman in a kimono—I like that better than a giant hunter," Emily said. "Do the Japanese have mythological stories about the stars?"

Toshi closed his phone app and turned to face Emily. "I think the stars were just used to reinforce imperial lineage and help emperors make decisions. Astrology, like many other things, was borrowed from the Chinese. I don't know that much about it."

"So people looked to the stars for answers?" Emily asked.

"Maybe there's a little of that. But why would you want to spend your whole life thinking about the future. There's the here and now," Toshi smiled.

"When I was in Kyoto, I kept trying to practice present moment awareness. It's the city of Zen. Sometimes I think I'm getting better at removing all the noise and negativity in my head. It must be wonderful to be a monk or someone that can notice their breathing and be totally calm all the time. Do you know a lot about Zen and inner peace?"

Toshi looked back out at the lake and nodded. "Something that has been very helpful to me is the concept of mono no aware. It's an acceptance that everything in life is coming to an end. It's a kind of sadness—a sensitivity to beauty. The impermanence of things makes them more valuable—more precious—sacred."

"So I'm supposed to think about things coming to an end?" Emily asked.

"When something is temporary, you stop to look at it and appreciate its beauty and importance. Life is constant change. To resist change is suffering. The wisest thing one can do is to live with a gentle sadness, aware that all things are passing."

"But I don't want to be sad," Emily smiled.

Toshi laughed. "It's a gentle sadness—and it helps you realize how beautiful life is. An ever so slightly wilting flower, a fading sound—sad and beautiful like Beethoven's Moonlight Sonata."

"What about happiness?" she asked.

"The beauty is the happiness."

Emily dropped her head and sighed. "When I got back from Japan, I was so depressed. I hadn't wanted my vacation to end. The people in Kyoto were so quiet, shy and friendly. It felt as if all my life I had been in the wrong place and then finally I was among my own kind of people. I came back home to noise and stress. I'm not like that. I'm not egotistical and competitive and self-obsessed. "

"You're very Japanese," Toshi smiled.

"My time in Kyoto came to an end. I'm not so sure I like the impermanence of things."

Toshi sighed sympathetically.

"Do the Japanese believe in reincarnation?" she asked.

"Traditionally, the Japanese have always struggled with the concept because it contradicts ancestor worship. However, some years ago we had our own version of a new age movement. It was called spiritual boom. Some people profited quite a bit with all the books and workshops and tours to collect mystical energy from so-called power spots. Supposedly, these power spots exist all over Japan and people used them to generate the energy they need to make their dreams come true. Interest faded, but after the 2011 earthquake and tsunami, people once again sought out spiritual things. But the Asian mind is inherently predisposed to think in terms of cyclical things."

"So you have this gentle sadness with you always?

"I try—and how about you? What are your coping strategies?"

Emily made a closed lip smile. "I've tried to play the supporting role. Now that I'm on my own, I can't look out for my younger brother. Whatever insecurities or lack of confidence I have, he's a million times worse. So maybe I bottle things up a lot. But I think my concern for my brother and trying to live my own life is helping me to grow. My highs and lows, my disappointments, it's all helping me to grow. You're helping me grow."

"I'm happy to be of service," Toshi smiled and was quiet for a moment. "So what you mean is that you're there for your brother, but not so much for yourself."

"Well, I hardly ever see him anymore. So I guess life is about me now."

"So what are you goals and aspirations?"

"Short or long term?"

"Both."

"I think in January, my new year's resolution will be to eat better—get a little more organized. Long term—maybe become a yoga instructor one day. What about you?"

Toshi looked out at the lake for a while. "I'd like to keep perceiving the world with gentle sadness, but hope that nothing too sad ever happens. But if something very sad were to happen, I hope that I remember to not bury the sadness within me. I hope that I will remember to go somewhere far away from other people and shout and throw punches in the air and do whatever it takes not to let any anxiety fester within me. Does that sound strange?"

"That sounds clever to me. You don't internalize negative emotions."

"The hardest thing is to remember to do that."

"Sometimes you forget?"

"Everyone gets their feelings hurt. They say that the key is not to suppress it—not to fight it. The more you resist something, the more you strengthen it. What's the worst that can happen—the feeling that your heart is beating out of your chest? You get that with exercise. You're not going to die because of it."

Emily took in a deep breath, wiped her eyes and smiled.

"Are you okay?" Toshi asked.

"I get emotional," Emily said.

"You have to be careful with those emotions," Toshi smiled.

"What a day," she said. "I saw Simeon talk this morning at Art Basel, and now I'm having this incredible conversation with you."

"But I'm better looking than Simeon."

"Yes you are," Emily laughed.

"So what kind of emotions are you feeling now?"

"Don't put a girl on the spot," she smiled.

"Too late."

"Well, the truth is I'm having a hard time with this gentle sadness stuff. I'm very happy now."

"So am I."

"I'm enjoying the moment—talking to you."

"You're very special, Emily."

"And so are you."

Emily looked up at the stars. "Do you think somehow an advanced alien civilization has figured out how to watch us and feel what we're feeling?"

"Maybe there's some kind of emotion telescope aimed right at us now."

"Do you think emotions have a frequency and travel out into space like radio waves?"

"I wonder."

"If there's such a thing as reincarnation, do you think we could be born in different worlds?"

"I suppose."

"I think I saw an anime movie like that once. The heroes hold hands so that they'll be reincarnated together and can continue to battle the forces of evil."

"We can hold hands—want to?" he smiled.

Emily put her hand in his. "So we'll be great warriors now, traveling through different dimensions together."

"It would be an honor to fight alongside you."

"But you're the one with samurai lineage."

"But you have super powers."

"I have super powers?"

"Yes, I have special vision that can detect super power. I noticed that you had it a long time ago."

Emily laughed. "What kind of super powers?"

"Power over the hearts of men."

"Oh really-"

"You didn't know?" Toshi smiled.

Emily stared out at the water for a while, blushing. "I've heard there's a Japanese custom—a lot of times it's the girl that asks the guy out on a date. But first she has to make some kind of confession."

"A kokuhaku."

"It's like hey, I like you, can we date?"

"Something like that."

"But we just met, so how does this work?"

"I'll take all the pressure off of you. Wanna go out on a date?"

"I would love to."

"How'bout next Saturday?"

"That would be great."

"Good."

"I don't know why—I thought maybe dating wasn't allowed in secret societies."

"Do you have any questions about the Koyosha?"

"Hmm—is there a dark net—anything cool like that?"

"Maybe," Toshi narrowed his eyes teasingly.

"So you have to bring me up to speed gradually-"

"What do you think of our group?"

"I like ghost stories. I get the feeling Father Osf's story was based on real life."

"I know," Toshi laughed.

Emily gave her phone an odd look. "This thing's acting funny again. It's got a mind of its own."

"What's wrong with it?"

"Apps keep opening and closing."

"-Could be hacked."

"I hope not," she sighed.

"Make sure you don't have bank or credit card information on it."

"I do all that from my laptop."

"Good."

Emily looked at Toshi for a moment. "So back to the group-"

"What do you want to know?"

"Whatever you can tell me."

"The best thing about our group is that it's so secret that nobody knows it even exists. So you can't ever tell anyone."

"I won't."

"Secret societies aren't so secret. Members get followed around, things get written about them. Conspiracy theorists go bananas over the so-called shadowy elite. But the Koyosha is invisible like a ghost. We even amuse ourselves by telling ghost stories. The truth is that there is serious business going on. We pick up where many private conferences and organizations leave off. There are several in our group who belong to the Bilderberg group. You may have heard of them—over a hundred and twenty people from Europe and North America that meet every year. A conservative and liberal from each country attend. They discuss politics and economics. Because the group is private, it scares a lot of people. Those who fear government are afraid that the conference is trying to form a world government. Those who fear the wealthy are afraid of capitalist oppression. People are afraid of the dark—afraid of what they can't see. It's for that reason that some people accuse the Bilderberg group of being the illuminati."

"Are they?"

"Of course not—the only true illuminati are you and me and all that exists in our secret world."

"Tell me again why I'm in this group?"

"Because you're well connected," Toshi smiled. "You know some very important people."

"I do," Emily laughed.

"Fate has brought us together."

"And what am I supposed to do?"

"You and I will be the next generation. Sit tight and absorb everything. Federico, Simeon and all the others—they'll show us how it's all done."

"How what is done?"

"How to deal with the things that go on in this world from a mystical perspective."

Emily furrowed her brow. "But isn't that what people fear—the social elite deciding things for everyone else?"

"Think of it as if you were going online to donate to a charity. You research different organizations until you find one that you think is worthy. Then you select a method of payment, enter a number and click the donate button. The ultra-wealthy do the same thing, but it's just a little more complicated."

"It's all philanthropic?"

"Mostly," Toshi nodded. "Unless something major comes up."

"Like what?"

"Stay tuned and see."

"So you guys are anonymous, mystical, wealthy, invisible people-"

"Not all are wealthy."

"Obviously, since I'm not."

"But you're a ghost, just like the rest of us."

"I told Simeon that I didn't want to be in this world."

"That's what probably did it."

"I was worried that he would think that I was suicidal."

"I'm sure he didn't think that. Context is everything."

"This almost seems like a weird dream," Emily made a happy sigh. "I came from Japan, fell into a funk, and now I'm here with people that like to tell Japanese ghost stories—soon to go out on a date with a Japanese man."

"Some things defy explanation," he said. "I can understand how you felt coming back from Japan. Not because America is a bad place, but it's easy to get discouraged by life. Most young people these days are very unhappy. I think it has something to do with having high expectations and believing that life will be somehow extraordinary or at least fun. But the reality is that most people hate their jobs—their lives are nothing like they thought it would be. There's nothing to get excited about."

"What about you? You're not in a job you hate."

"That doesn't mean there weren't times when I could find no meaning or purpose in life."

"And how did it all change?"

"Mono no aware."

"Tell me more about—mono awa-rey-"

"In the west, ideas about beauty are based on the characteristics of objects. Is it perfect? Does it have linear continuity and movement? Does it encompass all the correct traits of an era in history? Can one say that it is truly an impressionist painting or renaissance sculpture? But if you look at things in more of a Zen-like manner, beauty is something happening inside the individual as he or she experiences the work of art or object from nature."

"So it's more of a subjective experience," she said.

"Yes."

"And what does mono no awa-re have to do with Zen?"

"In Zen there is a longing for the eternal. The temporary is like the negative space in a photograph. Nothingness is proof that there is something."

"I'm not sure I follow."

"In other words, things don't last," he said. "What is left is emptiness. In the emptiness there is mystery and wonder."

"What's the mystery?" she asked.

"The eternal and infinite—don't you want to know what it is?"

"Yes."

"That happens inside of you."

"The beauty of things depends on how I feel about them."

"Exactly—if you were to ask Father Osf, he would tell you that the infinite is the mystery of Christ—cosmic Christ consciousness. If you were to ask Federico Jafet, he would tell you that the universe is his lover. They are best friends and mystics."

"And what about you—what do you think the infinite is?

"I see the infinite in your eyes," Toshi smiled.

"I'm serious," she laughed.

"So am I. The answers are within you."

"I think there's just a lot of crazy in me," Emily shrugged.

"Why do you say that?"

"When I got back from Japan, I kept thinking about stuff from anime and manga. Uhhh—let's just say that I was losing it."

"Losing your mind is good sign," Toshi smiled. "It can mean you're on the verge of something big."

"That's what Simeon told me, but I wonder if he was just trying to be nice."

"He wasn't just trying to be nice. I wouldn't worry about it."

Toshi scrolled through a menu on his phone and selected an mp3 file, placed the phone on the pier and stood, extending his hand to Emily. Soft piano notes accompanied by the voice of Robyn Rihanna Fenty radiated out over the surface of the lake.

"Can I have this dance?" Toshi asked.

"Of course," Emily smiled.

*...Makes me feel like I can't live without you...*

They slow danced under the starry sleeve of the kimono.

*...Round and around, and around, and around we go...*

"I just wanted to put my arms around you once before you leave,"

Toshi said.

"I don't want to go," she said.

"But you're tired."

"I'm exhausted."

"So next Saturday?"

"I want to stay—like the song."

"Me too."

"Okay. If anything happens to me, I'm going to come back and haunt you like a ghost."

"Like the one in your story?"

"That's right," she smiled.

"I'd be all right with that."

"I'll come and say boo."

"You know, we've met before," Toshi narrowed his eyes.

"We have?"

"Yes, in China of all places."

"I've never been to China."

"I'll explain it all to you next Saturday. We have so much to talk about."

# CHAPTER ELEVEN

Four Months before the Murder

Ulysses Garcia lived with his wife and stepson in a two bedroom apartment in Pembroke Pines. Ten months into his marriage, he had found that he was unable to cope with the moodiness and passive aggression of his wife, Melanie. Her affronts grew more brazen with time until her hostilities became only diminutively passive. His long hours at work were a source of resentment and yet part of him welcomed his time away from his predicament.

At home, he liked to spend most of his time at the computer tuning out his wife with headphones, although she would sometimes tap him on the shoulder and pull out an ear bud to inform him of her unhappiness. When her tirades would become unbearable, he would go to the shooting range and fill paper targets with holes. He would proudly display the black silhouettes both at home and at work.

Ulysses was reading about conspiracy theories one night when he came upon the podcast of a man named Nestor Turk. After a few hours of his ranting, he was addicted. Turk had managed to make sense of the world, revealing the reason for all chaos and suffering. Ulysses felt himself caught up in an epic battle of good versus evil. With new confidence, he began to talk back to Melanie, raising his voice and eventually becoming verbally abusive.

Over time, Ulysses changed his appearance to match Turk. He parted his hair and gained over forty pounds. He would come home from work with leftovers from a large lunch packed in polystyrene containers, walk past his wife and stepson, turn on his computer and navigate to the Nestor Turk website. There were a few videos, but mostly podcasts that kept him intrigued and entertained for most evenings.

Eventually, his need to be more like Turk caused him to vocalize his inner dialogue and emotions to a captive audience. His wife and stepson could only stare at him in bewilderment while his large frame blocked the television as he did his best to impersonate his internet idol. Melanie could plainly see his attempt to make his voice more guttural and raspy. She had seen one of Turk's videos on YouTube and could only shudder with pity and wonder if Ulysses was going through a faze or actually losing his mind. She tolerated his behavior for several weeks until she became convinced that he would not naturally let go of this obsession on his own.

One evening, Melanie thought to interrupt Ulysses hoping to interject rational thought and gradually deprogram his mind.

"The water is not being poisoned," Melanie said.

"Yes it is!" Ulysses snapped back. "The elite have been trying to poison and sicken us for a long time. They're trying to reduce the population. They're sterilizing us! There's a planetary police state. They're using food and water to wipe us out. I'm not eating anything you buy from the grocery store!"

"So you eat restaurant food? Where do you think they get the ingredients?"

"I'm buying this stuff from someone I trust."

"There's someone you trust?"

"This is no laughing matter! The water we drink is filled with fluoride to sterilize us and make us susceptible to mind control."

"Mind control?"

"The Nazis used it in concentration camps to make the prisoners more docile-"

"Oh my God," Melanie rolled her eyes.

"But worse, it's part of a population reduction program. They want to reduce the world population by eighty percent."

"Who's they?"

"The global elite."

"What global elite?"

"I don't see the point in talking to you. You don't get it!"

"Look, I get there are a lot of unhealthy foods. They use way too many chemicals. There are hormones in the meats. It causes early puberty in children. Pharmaceutical companies make stuff with lots of side effects. There are toxins in the soil. I get all that. But it's just corporations trying to make money by cutting corners—not some mysterious group of people who want to brainwash and sterilize the world."

Ulysses shook his head. "All that bad food you're eating is lowering your IQ. Let me explain everything to you. Maybe you have just enough intelligence to understand some of what I'm going to say."

Melanie shot back an angry look but didn't say anything.

"The Masons," Ulysses said. "They're taking over all the governments. And then the illuminati will take over the Masons. Actually, they're already controlling the Masons. The illuminati are an ancient satanic religion. It predates Christianity and Judaism. Its goal is to create hell on earth—a new world order. After they exterminate us all, the elite few will have the entire planet to themselves. These people are evil. They're poisoning our food and water and even spraying us with biological agents!"

Melanie raised her eyebrows. "What agents?"

"What do you think all the contrails in the sky are? That's all the shit they're dropping on us from airplanes. They have actual photographs of barrels on the wings of planes. No one is making this stuff up—it's real! So—anyway—the illuminati means those who have received light. Lucifer means light giver. You see how satanic this is?"

"I wish you'd care more about your family and stop wasting your time with all this nonsense."

"What—you want me to sit down with my family and watch TV? The media is made up of six corporations that feed you programming to distract you and keep you from what truly matters. You're the one that's caught up in nonsense!"

"Yules—my God! Do you hear what you're saying? Yules—honey, you're paranoid and delusional. I don't know how else to say it."

"If you only knew what you were being fed through the media," Ulysses scowled. "You're being brainwashed and controlled."

"How—how am I being controlled?"

"They do it in a lot of different ways. One is all the satanic symbols that are hidden in movies and concerts and on the news. The other is predictive programming. Secret societies prepare us for coming events by subliminally desensitizing us."

Melanie was visibly losing her patience. "So all this is going on while I'm watching television-"

"Take 9/11, for instance. They planned it for many years. So they got the masses ready for it by telling us what was going to happen in movies. The overpass in the Terminator movie—it says caution 9-11. The Beverly Hills Cops movie—the dates, 9-11 on the computer screen. The movie, The Patriot—9 pounds 11 ounces! The Big Lebowski—he's writing a check and dates it September eleven! The album by Supertramp, Breakfast in America—if you look at it in the mirror the numbers 911 appear over the twin towers! And now they're getting us ready for the next major event. I don't know what it is, but it always seems to have something to do with the number eleven. Nestor Turk believes that eleven is the number of chaos and disaster. It's not ten, a perfect number. But it tries to be greater than ten, like Lucifer trying to be greater than God."

"Yules! You're scaring me."

"Listen to me! Secret societies base their beliefs on Jewish mysticism—the kabbalah. Nestor Turk says that the number eleven in the kabbalah represents the element of air. The New Testament—in the book of Ephesians—says that Satan is the prince of the power of the air. There are dark evil things going on that we can't understand-"

"Eleven-"

"Yes, eleven! The twin towers stood like the number eleven. If you add up the numbers nine plus one plus one, you get eleven! The construction of the World Trade Center took eleven years! "Look at the Japanese tsunami— March 11th, 2011. The illuminati are behind it all! The illuminati—the enlightened ones—they have all the secret knowledge. They communicate with the fallen angels—demons. They're the aliens or interdimensional beings—whatever you want to call them?"

"Aliens?!"

"Aliens! —the grays and the reptilians. The illuminati want to enter into an age of communication with higher forms of intelligence."

Melanie's eyes were brimming with tears. "You're completely out of your mind."

"Truth is truth! You cannot argue with truth," Ulysses said.

"Disaster is coming and we must prepare for it."

Melanie sat next to her frightened son, her shoulders slumped and head hanging in dismay. "I don't care if you believe all these things, but I don't like having a gun in the house. I've been meaning to talk to you about it for a long time."

"Have you not heard a word I've been telling you? Ulysses said. "Society is going to completely break down. All the financial institutions and corporations are going to collapse. There will be wide spread killing and looting. Cities will burn to the ground. Hell on earth—hell on earth! There will be epidemics and famine. That's what they want—most of the human race dead! And then the elite class will inherit the earth. We need to protect ourselves."

"I wish I had a husband who was brave," Melanie said with trembling lips. "All I ever wanted was a brave and confident man. Instead I've got a coward. Why are you so afraid?"

Ulysses eyes bulged with anger. He went back to his computer and found an email notification in his inbox announcing a new Nestor Turk video. He clicked on the link and a website loaded in a new browser tab. There was a media player embedded after a block of text. Ulysses decided he would watch the video first and then read the article later. He enlarged the video full screen and Turk's gloomy face appeared, inhaling dramatically and shaking his head with grief.

"Hello, my friends," Turk said. "Things are much worse than you can ever imagine. I've been going through a lot of declassified documents. We now have secret police under federal control watching us to determine if we are subversive or enemies of the new world order. If they can find any tendencies in an individual towards rebellion against tyranny, they'll subliminally encourage violence and civil unrest through the programs we watch on TV. They want this so that they'll be able to institute martial law. The global banking elite of course are behind all of this—the illuminati and the extraterrestrials. These are all demonic forces. If they weren't evil, there would be no hunger or poverty. The illuminati are powerful enough to end all human suffering. But suffering persists because it's what they want. They're keeping technology and information from us. They won't let us see things from the fourth dimension as they do. They want all light and knowledge to themselves. Eventually, some alien human hybrid will pronounce that it's from the blood lineage of Jesus Christ in order to declare himself king of the world. This, of course, will be the anti-

Christ. Friends, we are living in the very end times. Interdimensional portals have been spotted over Norway and Thailand. Keep your eyes on the skies, my friends. That is where evil is coming. The devil is the prince of the air. Keep your eyes on the sky…"

Ulysses, completely enthralled by the apocalyptic spectacle, didn't notice that Melanie had put her son to bed and called the associate pastor at their church.

"Is everything all right?" he asked.

"No—I don't think so," she replied.

"What's wrong?"

"It's Ulysses—I'm worried about him."

"Why—is he okay?"

"He thinks the water is poisoned and planes are spraying toxic agents and we're all being sterilized-"

"Sterilized? Why does he think this?"

"It's all stuff he finds on the internet."

"Oh—I see. Has he been under a lot of stress lately?"

Melanie glanced over at Ulysses and bit her lip. "I don't think so."

"Nothing different at work? Does he have a stressful job?"

"He's a network administrator for a technology company. He practically lives on the computer."

"Well, I can give you the name of a counselor. A lot of people recommend this person. Perhaps Ulysses is just going through a phase. A lot of things online can seem real. If someone has an obsessive personality, sometimes they can take things a little too seriously."

"You think it's just a phase?"

"I don't know, but I'll certainly pray for you and your family."

The pastor gave Melanie the number of a local psychologist and they both said goodnight. Melanie stared out the sliding glass doors into the night, watching red brake lights in the distant traffic. She thought about what would be a good day to bring up counseling. Perhaps the weekend—she was too tired to do it that night.

Ulysses walked into the living room. "I know what I need to do."

"What's that?" Melanie asked.

"I'm going to use my God-given gifts to fight back," he said.

"How are you going to do that?" she asked.

"I'll create a computer virus to destroy the enemy."

"Be careful you don't destroy the world," she said with a hint of sarcasm.

"I wish I had a little more support from you," he said.

Melanie shrugged and sighed.

"I'm going for a walk," he said.

"Where are you going?"

"I just need to think about the malware I need to write. I think I'll call it the sore worm. It's been a long time, but I'm really excited about this. Malware, spyware—there's so much I can do. First, I could create a cavity virus to hide everything and then knock out antivirus software, then have it replicate like crazy. Once I get a sense of what's really going on in the world, I can create more viruses to go in for the kill."

"Be careful outside," she said. "They're spraying toxic agents."

"Go to hell."

Ulysses slammed the door and descended the stairs of the apartment building, the night cool after an evening rain. Ulysses was unaware that the sidewalks were reflecting the streetlights and the shadows of tree branches shaking in the breeze. He was unaware of the silver lining of the moonlit clouds gradually receding to a clear night. He was unaware of the sounds of laughter coming from children playing in one of the houses.

In his mind, Ulysses held the image of Nestor Turk raging his paranoid discourse into a microphone. The Federal Reserve System, the Rothschild family, Wall Street, the resignation of Pope Benedict XVI, HAARP, the Trilateral Commission—theories, plots and the suppression of secret knowledge all formed the threads of a perfectly woven tapestry of doom.

Every shuddering molecule in Ulysses' body tried to warn him that his brain had been commandeered by the specter of fear and deception. But all that resembled reason was hopelessly cast off like chaff from wheat. The dry scaly husks floated away as valueless proof of an ordinary world. He desperately wanted to suppress all logic and wisdom, afraid that passion, purpose and meaning would be plunged into oblivion.

The faces of rage, protests, riots, explosions and corpse-filled streets flashed inside of him. Wherever there was a crisis or a political hotspot, a sensational tragedy that the media would converge upon, this reality would trump all other realities. The quiet stillness of the neighborhood after the rain was only an illusion. To Ulysses, the greater reality was an impending disaster that was about to strike.

For the first time, he noticed the night. The smiling half-moon felt to him as if it were mocking his thoughts. He considered the possibility that it was transmitting something into his brain. He fought back by quoting Habakkuk, "The stones of the wall will cry out, and the beams of the woodwork will echo it!"

The next morning he heard his alarm clock broadcasting what seemed like the unintelligible voice of a man on the radio. He turned over in bed and reached out to press the snooze button but realized that it was only 5:50am. The alarm wouldn't go off for another ten minutes. He sat up.

"That's strange."

"What's strange? Melanie yawned.

"I was hearing voices."

Melanie covered her head with the pillow and sighed.

"It has started," he said. "They must somehow know about my plans."

"—Your plans to infect the world with a computer virus?"

Ulysses stared at the alarm clock glow on the ceiling. "Maybe. Did you know that during the attempted assassination of President Reagan, Hinckley got off six shots in three seconds? One bullet ricocheted off the limo, hit the president's rib and continued to tumble, just narrowly missing his heart?"

"No," Melanie said. "Why are you thinking about this?"

"Don't you find it fascinating?"

"No—not at all."

"The president usually wears a bullet proof vest. But for some reason, he wasn't wearing it that day. The bullet that got him caused one of his lungs to fill with blood. He would have been dead in twenty minutes. When they got him to the hospital, he collapsed right there in the lobby. The emergency room surgeons tried to stop him from bleeding to death, their hands shaking because it was the president. Congress stopped all its sessions. Wall Street suspended trading. This was some major shit-"

"This is the first thing out of your mouth in the morning?" Melanie said incredulously.

"-You know what really happened?"

"What?" she said in annoyance.

"Mind control—they got to Hinckley. Vice President George H. Bush was a member of the Skull and Bones, a secret society, and was once the director of the CIA. The Bush and Hinckley families were friends and rich oil people from Texas. They wanted Reagan dead so that Bush could be president. Why? —because Bush is a reptilian alien."

"Oh no-"

"There is actual video of George Herbert Walker Bush shape shifting and making all kinds of serpent sounds. These things are real and they're among us—pure evil."

"You said you heard voices this morning?" Melanie asked.

"Yes, but I'm not crazy. It could be that the grays or the reptilians were talking and didn't realize that I was awake yet."

"Aliens in this bedroom?"

"Somewhere in the fourth dimension."

"Look—don't get upset with me. Pastor Bill gave me the number of someone that does counseling."

"You called Pastor Bill?" Ulysses said angrily.

"Yes, but-"

"I can't believe you did that!"

"I'm worried-"

"Shut up! Shut up!"

"I'm getting up. It's almost six anyway."

Melanie went to the bathroom. Ulysses turned to look at the green LED numbers of the alarm clock, straining to hear whatever sounds or voices he had heard before. There in the emerald lights, he noticed something.

"It has always been there," he said to himself.

# CHAPTER TWELVE

Ulysses was driving back home from the gun range one day. His mind was so active that his thoughts spilled out into spoken words. When stopping at a red light, he would cover his mouth with one hand so that other drivers wouldn't see him talking to himself. The cameras over the traffic lights troubled him. He counted six video cameras at one crossing and one driver to his left that was staring at him.

"What are you looking at?—you piece of shit," he said through the closed driver's side window. "It's bad enough they have all this surveillance, I don't need some asshole looking at me too."

The light turned green and Ulysses accelerated. Once he was far enough from major intersections and other drivers, he resumed talking to himself.

"I'm the coward? She calls me a coward? Most people are scared shitless, but they won't admit it. They're absolutely miserable—living miserable lives. I've never met anyone that was happy. Everyone is miserable. And yet no one wants their misery to end. They're afraid to die. I don't want to die either, but I'll give my life for a cause. Maybe I should start will all these traffic light cams. They only increase traffic accidents. Everybody is slamming on their brakes whenever they see a yellow light—what a mess it creates. They're making so much damn money from the cameras. Imagine the guy who won the contract to supply the city with all the equipment. God—how much kickback is he getting? The Mayor probably gets a lot of it too.

"Maybe I could write a virus to fry all those mother boards—anything having to do with that. But it would take time away from what I really need to concentrate on—battling the evil scum. I'm sure they're behind all the surveillance cameras anyway. One day you won't be able to walk into your own bathroom without someone watching you. Shit, they're probably listening to me right now. If you're hearing this—I will get you before you get me!"

Ulysses heaved a sigh. "I can't even speak out loud! This sucks! Well, since you're on to me—since I have your attention, let me give you a piece of my mind. You can't have my soul! You can't have it!"

Traveling at fifty miles an hour on a trajectory to cross with Ulysses was a slightly inebriated man texting on his 5.5 inch screen. The man couldn't control the urge to finish a sentence and typed three last words. Then, his entire being seemed to pour itself into the need to send an attachment. A millisecond turned into a moment as he scrolled through his picture gallery.

As Ulysses crossed the intersection, the impact and flying glass sent his mind into hyperawareness, time slowing to the point that he could almost watch the shards moving through the interior of his car. He even had time to consider his entire world view. It came to him as the cliché of life passing before his eyes. An impression seemed to be encoded over the many things that were streaming past him. *I was right all along*, was the sum statement of his psyche.

Although Ulysses had no spinal injuries, paramedics immobilized his neck with a cervical collar and took him to the hospital. He was informed that he would require surgery to stabilize the fractured tibia and fibula in his left leg. Two days later, he was sliced open on a traction table and clamped. A guide wire was hammered through the gaping wound. Then a massive distractor was placed next to the leg so that nails could be inserted.

Ulysses awoke in the post-anesthesia care unit where hospital staff monitored his vital signs. The high-dose epidural opioids and anti-inflammatory agents caused the twilight of his consciousness to burn away and reveal a dark and daunting night. The voices were just outside the room, faceless entities scouring the internet and conferring like lawyers in the judge's chamber.

*He wasn't supposed to survive the accident. We can't kill him here—not in a hospital. He's being watched—heart rate, blood pressure, respiratory rate—temperature. But we can still keep him quiet. He doesn't think anyone knows about his crimes. We know everything he's ever done, every microorganism on every hair and flake of skin. We know about the immoral activities he was involved in with family members. We know about the bed-wetting, the twisted fantasies, the auto-erotic obsessions, voyeurism, fetishism, animal abuse—we know everything. Look—right here is a link. It's all been documented. Once he's out of the hospital, we'll kill him. What does this piece of trash think he can do to us? Did he really think that he could send an internet bot to find us? Did he think he would be able to destroy us with a computer virus? All we have to do is tell the police about him. We'll frame him for something. Or we could just kill him—either way we win. Decisions, decisions…*

Upon being released from the hospital, Ulysses remained quiet and kept his auditory hallucination a secret from Melanie. She wanted to stay home with him for at least a day, but he had insisted that she not miss work. In bed alone with a laptop, he began to search for weaknesses in his enemy's kingdom. Using an anonymous browser proxy service, he tried to hide his internet activity as best he could. He was unable to find any obvious portals into secret societies, so he decided to at least get started on designing a computer virus. In the course of his research, he stumbled upon many types of surveillance software made available for all types of devices.

The pain killers kept the voices present but indecipherable. Ulysses would stop his work to search the web with such keywords as *listening to the fourth dimension* and *preventing an assassination*. The searches related to the fourth dimension produced results that explored a type of geometry that was temporal. It was an important distinction to understand the difference between the temporal and time. The universe was made of the spatial and temporal, bending and stretching—antimatter actually going backwards in time—interesting, but little to do with voices just beyond his grasp.

The result for *preventing an assassination* had more to do with the US secret service and a plethora of JFK articles. Irritated, Ulysses made an advanced search with the words *how to prevent my murder*. This only returned results for killers that had made the news and even guides to committing the perfect murder. Finally, he queried the simple question: how to protect myself from a killer. Don't talk to anyone. Be aware of your surroundings. Lock your doors. It all seemed like worthless advice. No doubt, a secret society would employ assassins that were a million times more deadly than any serial killer.

He noticed the browser tab with fourth dimension results still open.

He pondered antimatter going backwards in time. What if he could be like antimatter? he mused. What if the world improved in the opposite direction? Pollution and progress would reverse course and soon he would find himself in the lush forests of North America, before the arrival of the Europeans, before the extinction of many trees and plant species. He would happen upon some natives living peacefully with nature. Was this what the secret societies wanted? Ulysses asked himself. The world as it once had been—the few communing with the infinite expanses of land, beauty and wonder?

Ulysses sighed with irritation. How on earth could he allow himself to think such thoughts? Perhaps the mind control was already at play. If they could get him to see things their way, there would be no need for violence. Ulysses knew what he had to do—save the billions of innocent people from genocide. There would be no element of surprise. He had heard the voices in the post op recovery room. They knew everything and would probably soon attempt to kill him. This he was absolutely sure of.

His only choice seemed to be to work hard and work fast. If he died by the end of the year, perhaps by then his cyber-attack would be wreaking havoc. It seemed to Ulysses that the most logical way to find a secret society would be to find secret money—no easy task. In Seychelles, an archipelago in the Indian Ocean, there exists shell companies. These companies within companies within companies are a hub of corruption and money laundering. If the social elite wanted to control the world through secret societies, much of their money would plausibly be hidden in offshore havens. The trillions of dollars in financial refuges—equivalent to the US, Chinese and Japanese economies combined—are hidden in spurious firms.

Ulysses had read about bank subsidiaries from foreign countries channeling untold amounts in bribes, operating illegal Internet companies, and governments all over the world flowing untraceable money through the Seychelles. The islands seemed to Ulysses as good as any other place to begin a search for the Illuminati. But how would he be able to hack into information ingeniously designed to evade detection? He was only one person. The North Koreans have two thousand cyber warriors—Bureau 121—stationed around the world, conducting attacks against perceived enemies. One thing was certain, he could model his attacks after the Bureau 121 malware infection of South Korean banks in 2013. Perhaps he would get lucky and find that a shell company within another shell company would lead him to one particular individual. Find this person and take down an organization.

If he hadn't been bedridden, he would probably be pacing around the apartment with excitement. Never had so many ideas popped into his mind at the same time. Without the offensive plan, his impending assassination would debilitate him with terror. There was a history of anxiety and paranoia in his family. It wouldn't take much to produce a full blown panic attack. Surely, the meds were working and keeping him calm. But how would he cope with knowing what was in store for him once the pain killers wore off? He had to tell someone about the voices he heard in the hospital, but whom? He couldn't tell Melanie. Telling her anything was the same as telling their pastor.

He reached for the bedpan and relieved himself. Then he drank more juice and chewed on some saltines. It soon became evident to him that he could strategize and brainstorm as much as he wanted, but that he wouldn't get much work done while on pain killers. He was too sleepy to concentrate. The carbohydrates worsened his drowsiness, so he closed the lid to his laptop and turned on the TV. The local news was on.

*Twenty year old white Hispanic male is wanted for questioning for multiple murders in Broward County. He was recently in an automobile accident and suffered a broken leg. He was treated at Florida Medical Center in Fort Lauderdale and released. The person, by the name of Ulysses, is said to have been present at several crime scenes and considered a person of interest. In Tallahassee, the governor today signed…*

Ulysses heard the sound of a key unlocking the door and recoiled in fear. Melanie had come home for lunch. She went straight to the bedroom to inspect his supply of food and medication.

"Did you hear anything strange on the news?" Ulysses said anxiously.

"No—why?"

"I don't know how to say this, but the police might come any second."

"The police—what's going on?"

"Someone is trying to frame me for a crime. They were talking about me on the news."

"They mentioned you by name?"

"Yes, right now I'm a person of interest, but you know that just means they're going to arrest my ass and put me in jail."

Melanie sighed. "Those are some really powerful pain killers they're giving you."

"I didn't imagine it!" Ulysses shouted.

"Look, I just wanted to check up on you. I have to get back to work. Don't watch anymore TV."

"You don't believe me—you never believe me!"

"Yules, if the police come, tell them that you just had a major operation and that you can't move. Tell them to call me."

"I'll do that, but don't turn off the TV."

"I really don't think-"

"Leave it on!"

"Fine," she said. "I really need to get going. Call me if there is any emergency."

After Melanie had left, Ulysses continued to watch the midday report.

*We have an update on the story about the man wanted for questioning in multiple Broward county homicides. His name is Ulysses Garcia. He's a network administrator working for NXP Webcasting in Pompano Beach Florida. He's described as a loner with a history of illegal firearms possessions. Immediate family describe Garcia as a bed-wetter, obsessed by auto-eroticism, voyeurism, fetishism and animal abuse. One person said that he was—quote—"a very sick individual." Sources close to the police investigation say that Garcia most likely stalked, raped and murdered several women in the greater Fort Lauderdale area within the last two years. If you have any information that can further aid police in this investigation you are urged to call Crime Stoppers…*

"I've never illegally possessed a gun! I've never killed anyone!" Ulysses shouted at the television.

He lifted the lid to his laptop and booted up again. "No one needs to know about my bed-wetting and all that stuff," he mumbled softly. Fighting the urge to sleep, he focused his attention on Seychelles. Hours went by in a hypnogogic state testing the security of servers and gleaning whatever information was easily accessible. A Japanese kanji appeared to him in the registration documents of several accounts.

"Of course," he said. "The Bank of Japan—they're part of the Trilateral Commission—North America, Western Europe and Japan…Japan…Japan."

He felt a presence next to him and turned to see Dwight D. Eisenhower shaking his head.

"President Eisenhower," Ulysses gasped.

"You can call me General," Eisenhower frowned.

"General-"

"You're a fat slob—an absolute disgrace. Drop and give me fifty pushups."

"I'm sorry. I just had surgery."

"I can't begin to tell you what a sorry lard ass you are. If I had more time with you—you'd be in for a world of hurt, soldier. I'm being transferred to the War Plans Division in Washington. Things are pretty hairy now with Pearl Harbor and all the chaos in the world."

"Oh, I see," said Ulysses. "You think it's 1941."

"Don't patronize me, you sack of shit! I know it's not 1941. Don't you understand any of this dimensional mumbo jumbo you've been reading about? They've got some parts of it right. You're the antimatter, retreating into the past. I'm going forward. Today we pass each other."

"I'm the antimatter?"

"Well, you're not normal matter! You're far from normal. You're an absolute disgrace. You need to start an exercise regimen and use some self-control at the dinner table. By the way, this plan of yours to destroy secret societies is ludicrous-"

"I saw your 1961 speech on YouTube. You warned us against the New World Order."

"You moron!" Eisenhower scowled. "I was warning people about the military industrial complex. I said that the potential for the disastrous rise of misplaced power exists. That had nothing to do with extraterrestrial aliens and secret societies or any other such nonsense. You're headed in the wrong direction, young man. You need to reevaluate your life. And another thing—what are you planning to do with that gun of yours?"

"It's my constitutional right to arm myself," Ulysses said with self-satisfaction.

"Listen carefully to me. I don't mind civilians owning guns, but you, young man are psychopath. Pay very close attention to what I'm about to tell you. I, Dwight David Eisenhower, am your one moment of sanity. We are going in opposites directions. We are meeting very briefly. This—for you—is a fleeting encounter with mental and emotional stability. That is what I represent. I strongly beseech you to do everything within your power not to bring harm to anyone. For

God's sake, seek counseling, talk to a pastor, find treatment at a mental facility—do something! For some people, a certain amount of spiritual insanity is beneficial—the passion of young lovers, the madness of creativity, the discarding of an old and pessimistic self and the attaining of new confidence and vigor. But you, young man, are just plain demented—deranged—an elevator that doesn't go to the top floor—a sleeve short of a sweater—several tacos short of a fiesta platter. I would smack you silly right now if I thought it would do any good. Well, I have to go. The future is waiting for me. It's been fascinating so far—flat screen televisions, mobile broadband internet access—driverless cars-"

There was a knock on the door.

"Ulysses, it's me, Pastor Bill."

"Hello?" Ulysses replied.

Pastor Bill entered the room with a warm smile and stood next to Ulysses' bed. "I thought I'd stop by to see how you're doing."

"The door was unlocked?" Ulysses asked.

"Melanie said she would leave it open for me, since you wouldn't be able to get up out of bed."

"The door was unlocked?"

"Yes, I hope that's okay."

"The door was unlocked."

"How are you feeling?"

"I can't believe the door was unlocked."

"If this isn't a good time, I can come back another day."

"I just can't believe that the door was unlocked."

"Are you feeling any pain?"

"No—no pain. I understand that we're under your pastoral care, but I'm really not feeling like playing along with all this—maybe another day."

"Absolutely—I just wanted to stop by and say hi."

"Thank you."

"We have you on the prayer list for your recovery. Take care."

"Bill."

"Yes-"

"Can I tell you something?"

"Sure—what?"

"Never mind."

"If there's anything you need to get off your chest-"

"No—nothing. I'm going to sleep now."

"All right, but if you need to talk, I'm always here."

"Thank you, Pastor Bill."

Ulysses sighed with relief the moment he heard the pastor close the door. Soon, his irritation returned when he remembered that the door was unlocked. He checked the Nestor Turk website for news headlines. A former World Bank Senior Council admitted that a second species on Earth controls money and religion—intelligent creatures, mathematical, not creative. They have elongated skulls, and may produce offspring with female humans, but the offspring is not fertile. A former Canadian Minister of National Defense said that there are at least four known alien species that have been visiting Earth for thousands of years.

Drive away in an all-new Nissan Altima for only one eighty nine a month! Or an all-new Nissan Versa for only one forty nine a month! The volume of the television commercial startled Ulysses. He lifted the remote control and pressed the power button. The room was silent except for the hum of the air conditioner. He listened carefully to see if he could hear any voices. He detected a soft mutter, but couldn't make out any words.

They hadn't come to arrest him, he thought. Perhaps the police captain had been given orders to stand down—orders from high up. They're going to take their time with this, he concluded. He typed the words into the stealth mode search engine: Emily Patrick ASMR videos.

# CHAPTER THIRTEEN

## Two Days after the Murder

Toshi Yamamoto stared at his tired eyes in the bathroom mirror. He had seen similar puffy dark circles on the faces of people who had been crying or were weary from life. He felt a strange frustration that the death of Emily had produced no tears in his eyes. If only he could have a good cry, then he would release the stagnant emotions, he thought.

Toshi looked at his reflection for a long time, his mind completely blank. He had spent years practicing the art of meditation and had developed the ability to quiet the mind. Reaching complete silence was something that pleased him, the fruit of countless of hours of effort. However, his current state provided nothing for him to take pleasure in. Even if his mind wandered, there was nothing to contemplate. All that he was left with was a profound existential emptiness that was both cruel and unfathomable.

He could still feel Emily in his arms slow dancing by the pier. If the tragedy of her passing hadn't left him feeling so numb, he could have meditated upon the memory of her touch and scent. Being able to see her face again was as simple as searching for her online. He refrained from doing so until what he perceived an adequate amount of time had gone by. But what would that amount be? A day—a week—that would fall away with all the hollowness he felt?

He went into the den, booted up his computer and clicked through thirty nine pages of thumbnails on YouTube. Unable to find Emily, he entered different key words that he had preferred not to use, ASMR black girl. His nondual way of thinking didn't like separating reality into fragments and labeling them. We are one consciousness. To say that Toshi was Asian and Emily was black was the most superficial perception possible. And yet, in this one instance, he referenced a color. How could that define anyone? How does one associate the manifestation of life as a single adjective? These thoughts along with the frustration of not being able to find Emily's YouTube channel were draining his resolve and attention.

After the new search, he found a still of one of Emily's videos. It hadn't been cropped properly and it was only the lower half of her face but he recognized her. He never would have guessed the name she had chosen, SoftEDPbot. Her initials, EDP, sandwiched between soft and bot. He selected the video and let out a sad breath when he saw Emily's face close up to the camera.

Hi, this is Ruth. I haven't done a whisper video in a while. I've done a few role-play ones lately, but this one will be whispered. It will be a role-play too. I'm sorry for being real. I should've just started with the role-play. Okay, forget I said that. Let's begin. Hi, what's your name...? Oh, all right. My name is Ruth and I'll be the one doing your facial today. Have you ever had a facial before…? Okay. I'm going to take off your makeup with some cotton balls. First, let me spray some makeup remover on the cotton ball.

Toshi clicked the pause button, and searched Emily's other videos until he came across one entitled My Strong Opinions. He selected it and saw Emily again, this time wearing a light denim shirt.

Hi everyone, this is Ruth. I just wanted to take a break from the usual role-play and whisper videos. Today, I'd like to just tell you what I think. I can't believe that anyone would actually care what I think, but I do get emails from people telling me that they would like to know more about me. No, my real name isn't Ruth. But I'm not going to tell you what it is yet—not until I feel more comfortable. I'm a very private person.

All right, so what do I believe? I believe that life is strange. I'm planning a trip to Japan. I've never been out of the country before, and I'm kind of nervous. I'm trying to relax, playing Hammock songs, binaurals and listening to other people's ASMR vids. How did I become an ASMRtist? I just happen to stumble across a few videos and wanted to know more about it. I somehow knew that I was meant to do this. I hope I don't get tired of it because I enjoy it so much. So, anyway, I'm spending a week in Kyoto. I can't wait to go to the International Manga Museum, and the temples and shrines. I've been researching the city. I know so much about it now and I just want to see it all in person.

I remember one of my first ASMR experiences happened while watching a video of a street in Kyoto with the cherry blossoms falling in slow motion. I felt the top of my head tingling. I was getting high off of the music. I felt so relaxed, like I had found all the answers to life and everything in the world was perfect. There were no more mysteries—maybe there were, but all the puzzle pieces fit together so well, that all there was left to do was enjoy. —spiritual calm, joy—peace. So, I had this odd feeling that one day someone would explain the falling of the cherry blossoms to me…

A short time later, Toshi was driving across the General Douglas MacArthur Causeway with a single thought piercing his consciousness. *I was the one that she was searching for. I—told her about mono no aware and the impermanence of all things. Emily became the most beautiful and impermanent thing I have ever known.*

He stopped at a convenience store, and with a heightened sense of awareness noticed everything. The grungy clothes of the men buying lottery tickets, the gleam of every item in the store wrapped in plastic, the cashier behind the counter. She reminded him a little of Emily. For a moment, he feared for her safety. Convenience store clerks are often victims of robbery and murder. This wasn't Japan. Anything could happen to her. He silently formed a prayer in his mind, please protect her.

Toshi met Simeon Suslov about an hour later for lunch at a Turkish restaurant by the beach. They liked the outdoor seating facing the ocean. They had practically made a ritual out of noting that most of the dishes on the menu seemed more Greek than Turkish, but that they would never say anything to the waiter. They both chose lamb wraps in tzatziki sauce and gave each other sad looks through sunglasses.

"I feel terrible," Toshi said.

"I know—so do I," Simeon replied.

"I hope the detectives are able to find something."

"I wish I could have been more helpful," Simeon said. "Imagine what they were thinking when I told them that I got drunk and didn't remember anything. They must have thought I had something to do with it."

"You weren't drunk," Toshi smiled. "When have you ever been drunk?"

"I told them that I was tipsy. It would have taken too long to explain everything. And it would have only confirmed to them that I was some kind of lunatic. The last thing I wanted was for them to think that."

The waiter came and took their lamb wrap orders and quickly returned with glasses of ice water.

Toshi held down a slice of lemon in his glass. "Explain everything to me. It might help me get my mind off things. I never get tired of hearing about your lunacy."

"But at least you understand me," Simeon laughed. "Of course, I wasn't even slightly tipsy after drinking the wine, but I had definitely been experiencing altered states of consciousness that evening. I knew what I was in the mood for."

"Veronica," Toshi said and made a closed lip smile.

"Yes, but very different from what one would think."

"You have to tell me in detail what goes on with you two."

"Very well," Simeon sighed. "We went to one of the guestrooms. We lay in bed together, side by side, facing up. And then we both had an energy experience."

"There was no touching?"

"At one point, yes, we held hands. Actually, I just wanted a hand to squeeze when things got intense."

"How long did it last?"

"One hour, but it's very exhausting."

"Both of you can do this?"

"Yes. It's both physical and not physical at the same time. It didn't take much time at all—quite effortlessly, we were both experiencing it. Just imagine the endorphin release, the neurochemicals flooding the brain. It really is a transcendent, euphoric event. One day, I think, there won't be a need for mind altering drugs or illicit sex or any of the vices that ruin people's lives. There'll be no need for men to cheat on their wives or the drug cartels to resort to violence. All pleasure will pale in comparison to what we can do to ourselves with only the use of our brains."

"What's to keep you from pulling that lever all day like the lab rats that choose cocaine over food?"

"Actually, that study was just a myth," Simeon said. "But what's true is that when we consume most medications—or do just about anything that is not natural—we're destroying our bodies."

"But everything you do is completely natural."

"Precisely. And consider all the bad decision many people are guilty of—the huge lapses of judgment all for the sake of cheap sex. All for what—a little tiny orgasm confined to one area of the body? You know they caught the Miami police chief on video with two undercover detectives posing as prostitutes-"

"I heard about it."

"And just the other day, they videotaped another officer engaged in something similar. Just imagine the humiliation—the trouble those men are in."

"A lot of people are just unhappy," Toshi said. "They just want to feel good, even if it's just for a moment—a moment that they will perhaps regret later, but nevertheless, they need that moment. What can be done? Most people simply aren't at that stage of human consciousness where they can achieve ecstatic bliss."

"I have to say that all the meditation and consciousness exploration I've done over the years has definitely been worth it," Simeon smiled.

"Being old isn't such a bad thing, I guess," Toshi said.

"I wouldn't mind being young again like you."

"You can't have everything, Simeon. You're living a life of rapturous experiences. So many have tried and failed."

"It's more than just experiences. I'm burning calories, increasing blood flow and mental sharpness. My cells regenerate. I'm slowing the aging process. Of course this is true for most orgasms, but we are talking levels above any ordinary experience. And most importantly, it's a gateway to enlightenment."

"I'm happy for you," Toshi said. "There's something about talking to someone who knows a little more—experienced a little more—that leaves me feeling hopeful. Both the role of student and the role of teacher have their unique joy. I felt a little like a teacher when I was talking to Emily. She was fascinated by me and Japanese culture. I was delighted to tell her everything I knew. For some reason we kept discussing impermanence."

"It must be tough," Simeon said.

"She did videos on YouTube. I watched a few of them. She described feeling tingling sensations and possibly what we might consider altered states of consciousness. I wonder if she was on the verge of a true spiritual awakening."

"She most definitely was," Simeon said. "I wonder how many there are like her. If we were a little more like the all-knowing and powerful people we're supposed to be. Eh—but we *are* one of the few true secret societies in the world. What's this obsession with the illuminati? There's no such thing as the illuminati. Well, it did exist in the 1700's, briefly, for about nine years in Bavaria. As for the Freemasons—what's so secret about it? There are millions of members. All you have to do is go to your local lodge and ask to join. Anyway, Emily was special."

"She was," Toshi said.

"We didn't need to become benevolent provocateurs, dropping hints and trying to entice her to come a little closer—there was no need for social engineering. It must have been meant to be. As they say, nothing happens by chance—but why her murder? It just doesn't make sense."

"It doesn't," Toshio shrugged. "In Japan, we are by nature quiet people. We don't have a lot to say when someone dies. Priests typically charge a fortune for a grave site at a temple and all the priestly duties they perform. And at such a time, the grief-stricken don't want to haggle. But now that the birth rate is falling, there will be very few to visit the graves and worship at the proper times. Some are even wondering what the need is for a grave if no one is going to visit. Wooden markers are beginning to replace the traditional stone ones. One day, everyone will be dead and there will be no one around to remember them. The wooden markers will decay and all things will recede into the void. When you care deeply for someone, you want them to be honored—to be remembered. But there are never words or sentiments of any sort to convey a person's magnificence. How do we deal with death? How do we remember Emily?"

"We have to deal with our feelings first," Simeon said. "Our souls need to somehow recover from the senselessness of it all."

"My grandmother would have thought that her death had something to do with karma. When something unnatural and inexplicable like this happens, the older generation thinks that it must have something to do with some cause and its effect. Our generation doesn't believe in these things so much. But not believing anything is hard. The mind desperately wants things to make sense."

"Perhaps we can do something for her family," Simeon said.

"Perhaps," Toshi agreed.

# CHAPTER FOURTEEN

Ryan Salter read the titles on the book spines as Detective Ramos searched Emily's bed. The other two detectives of the homicide team, Rob Ostroff and Hector Noriega, were also in Emily's apartment hoping to find something that would cry out to them like blood from the ground. Rob and Hector were more interested in Emily's electronic devices.

"There's no sign of a significant other," Ramos said.

Salter grabbed a book off the shelf. It contained the movie art of Hayao Miyazaki. He leafed through the pages of storyboard and concept art for Studio Ghibli films and then returned the book to its place next to Emily's collection of Haruki Murakami novels.

"I keep thinking that Emily has left us so many clues that we're not seeing something because it's almost too obvious," Salter said. "I don't want to let her down."

"We won't," Ramos said.

"Are we doing a disservice to the case by pulling an all-nighter? Would a couple of hours of sleep help our brains see something we're not seeing?"

"Emergency room surgeons do it."

"That's insane. I wouldn't want someone operating on me that's been working a twelve hour night shift."

Salter looked at the 2011 Tōhoku earthquake and tsunami relief poster. Under the red Japanese sun was the date 3/11/11. He turned to Detective Ostroff who was sitting on the floor examining Emily's laptop.

"Anything?" Salter asked.

"Good thing we asked the cybercrime unit to check her phone for malware," Ostroff said. "Someone installed something and then deleted it—removed it at the time of the murder—I think our killer hacked into her phone, stalked her, strangled her and then erased the surveillance software. It's too bad they couldn't recover anything. We can bring the laptop back to the station, but all the killer really needed was the phone to invade her privacy."

"This is everything required to shoot her YouTube videos," Detective Noriega said. "—A tripod, a 3D microphone, her laptop for editing and this strange little thing."

Noriega held up a Sony Action Cam.

"Underwater camera?" Salter asked.

"It's got a water resistant casing, but it's actually designed more for action sequences," Noriega said. "It's the type of camera that you mount to your helmet when shooting surfing or skateboarding videos. I don't know why she would be using this type of camera for an ASMR channel."

"It's the wrong tool for the job?" Salter asked.

"Yeah—it's a bit odd."

"No skateboarding videos or anything like that on her laptop," Ostroff said. "All her videos are ASMR."

"She was too old for skateboarding," Ramos said. "A girl her age would need something like that if she was shooting a chase scene in a movie with the camera strapped to the front of the car—if she were a filmmaker."

"Her thing was video blogging," Noriega said.

"The victim didn't have a lot of money," Salter said. "She must have saved every penny she had for the trip to Japan. Are those 3D microphones expensive?"

"This one looks pretty expensive—maybe around five hundred," Ostroff said. "Good mikes are expensive. This one might be sold especially for ASMR—low self-noise and all that."

"Could they be gifts?" Salter asked.

"Well, we could find out where it was purchased and to whom it was sold," Noriega said.

"Find out about the Action Cam as well. She probably didn't buy that herself, since it's the wrong type of equipment to have for what she was doing."

"You got it," Noriega said.

"How was her family?" Salter asked.

"They took it hard," Noriega said ruefully.

"Such bad news," Salter shrugged.

"Here's something," Ostroff said. "One of her videos on the hard drive is named Do_Not_Post.wmv. It's probably not on her channel."

"Let's see it," Salter said.

Ostroff double clicked the file and Emily appeared in a khaki t-shirt, smiling at the camera.

Today, I'm going to answer questions that people emailed me. One person wrote me—what do you do about the creeps that say mean things? …I can just ignore them. If they keep being mean, I can just delete their comments. Also, I can always block them on YouTube. Although there are a lot of mean people out there, the ASMR community is very nice. It's the outsiders that stir up all of the trouble. One day, I think human consciousness will outgrow the need for meanness and cruelty. Just like adolescents eventually grow up, the human race will mature and stop acting like juveniles. That's just what I think. Hopefully, the human race is just a troubled teen. I prefer not to think about the implications of the human race being like a depraved sociopath. You've heard the stories about all the serial killers that were never quite right in the head, even as children. I hope the human race isn't that kind of race. I hope the human race is the kind that is just going through an awkward unhappy stage but will eventually mature into adulthood. That's what I hope. Okay—I'm rambling. Next question…

Salter and Ramos were driving to Pompano Beach, Emily's voice echoing in their heads.

"We have seventy five thousand potential suspects," Salter said.

"Possibly more," Ramos said. "That's just her channel subscribers. That's not counting all the people who have watched her videos without subscribing."

Salter sighed. "And I thought this would be an easy case. We had her phone. Her phone led us to Simeon Suslov. I thought it was going to be that simple. I kind of knew that he wasn't the one the moment I saw him. Usually, it's some loser nut job, not a guy giving a speech about fine art to all the Art Basel crème de la crème. So what do we have? —A body surrounded by creepy drawings of ancient Asian lion-dogs, torn out and arranged almost in a ritualistic manner. The victim is a beautiful black girl with all her clothes carefully removed. She was strangled after the blunt force trauma to the head probably caused her to become unconscious. The perp had been cyberstalking her. That night, the vic was initiated into a secret society. That very night, she's murdered. The perp got her when she was going home. Was there something about the The Hermetic Order of the Mystic Koyōsha that offended our perpetrator? They assembled, told ghost stories and socialized. Then she meets Toshio and a new relationship appears to be blossoming. Could the perp have overheard the entire conversation? The malware on her phone could have activated the microphone, maybe even the camera if the phone was pointed in the right direction. Maybe the perp was in love with the vic. The romance makes the perp go into a jealous rage. He has complete access to her phone's GPS, tracks her and somehow gets her to go for a stroll in the park with her. Obviously, she knew him. Then he hits her with something and strangles her while unconscious. She's been the object of his desire for a long time. He needs to see her naked. He strips off all her clothes just to take in her beauty one time. He doesn't violate the body in any way, because in his mind, he's in love with her. He removes the malware from the phone and tosses it on the ground. So who is this guy?"

"The bruising on the neck indicates it's probably a male," Ramos said.

"We need to find out more about her social life—who her friends were. Did she have any guy friends that she was close to? Anyone that she rejected—perhaps someone that just wasn't in her league? The shit women have to deal with-"

"I know—it's easy for guys," Ramos smiled. "Unless you're a celebrity, no woman is going to obsess over any man. And statistically, there are more male homicidal maniacs."

Salter nodded in agreement. "Over ninety percent of homicides in the US are committed by males. We go to where Emily Patrick worked and see if we can find our weirdo. My hunch is that it was a coworker. She wouldn't have a friend like that. This person was too beneath her, in my opinion."

"Since when are you so judgmental?" Ramos laughed. "What's all this about some people being better than others?"

"We're talking murdering scum," Salter said. "He's beneath all of us."

"We just do our jobs, but aren't most of these people mentally ill? What might we be capable of if our brains were damaged?"

"All right—the perp had life breathed into them by God. They were created innocent children and the breath in their lungs is from heaven. But they are mental scum. Good hardware, infected software."

"Ah, the computer analogy-"

"You know what I can't get out of my head?"

"What?"

"The story that Emily told—Simeon said that a jealous female ghost had tried to kill her. What kind of story is that to tell the night of your murder? —A self-fulfilling prophecy?"

"It happens. Look at the people in Waco. They were brainwashed by their cult leader to believe that the end of the world was coming. It most definitely came for them. I wonder if it has ever occurred to any of those people that are constantly obsessing and worrying about something that all this foolishness might actually cause something bad to happen."

"So you think that Emily was killed by a ghost?"

"No."

"Do you believe in ghosts?"

Salter smirked. "Hmm—I'm not answering that."

"Why not?"

"Detectives don't talk about things like that."

"Why? Because it would make our job creepier than it already is?"

"Yeah, that's pretty much the reason."

"Have you ever seen a ghost?"

"I'm not talking about that," Salter laughed.

"Oh, come on. I'm new to this. Tell me what there is to know just once, and I'll file it away in the back of my head and never mention it again."

"You're very persistent, Salter sighed." "Okay—I'm going to say this just once and it will never be discusses or repeated."

"I promise."

Salter tapped on the steering wheel for a moment. "One evening, many years ago, I looked—for the first time—at a wall covered with photographs of corpses. Their eyes were open, and at first, I didn't realize that they were murder victims. I just thought they were pictures of living people. The moment I comprehended that I was staring at the dead, a dark shadow walked right past me and left the room. There was another police officer sitting at a desk looking at his computer. He didn't notice the shadow. And I wasn't going to say anything. I thought about it for a long time. Was it a hallucination? I had never seen anything so real—so plain and simple. Who or what this spirit was intrigued me. Are ghosts repulsed by such photographs? Was this a spirit that had always been with me and had fled when I saw the eyes of something that hit too close to home? Or was it the ghost of one of the murder victims? I guess I'll never know. So there you have it—another ghost story. This stays between you and me."

"I'll never breathe a word," Ramos said.

"Never."

"Never."

"Back to our victim," Salter said. "Her co-workers have been informed of her death. The shock may just be starting to wear off—so we question those who worked most closely with her. If anything seems unusual to us, we go in with all our faculties and over analyze if necessary...Chinese lion-dog drawings, a secret society and a cyber-stalker—her story about a ghost that tried to kill her. I hope that's not what this is. I hope we're not dealing with someone that's so good that they're like a phantom killer. So far, there's no evidence except that he deleted spyware from the victim's phone. That's the only clue that suggests the killer is human, although not much of a human."

"Are you going to mention the Mystic Koyosha?" Ramos asked.

"I would hate to be the one to blow the lid off a secret society," Salter said. "If I can help it, the secret will stay a secret, unless the Koyosha is essential in making a case. They seem like nice people. I wouldn't mind belonging to a club or something like that."

"Why's that?"

"I've got too many skeletons in the closet and too many enemies in the department."

"I'm sorry, that's none of my business."

"I trust you, Detective Ramos. I do."

"Because you're a great judge of character?" Ramos smiled.

"Exactly."

# CHAPTER FIFTEEN

Salter and Ramos knocked on the glass door of NXP Webcasting and held up their badges. The receptionist at NXP Webcasting saw them and the door unlocked with a buzzing sound. The two entered the lobby and walked up to the front desk.

"Hi, I'm Detective Ryan Salter of the Fort Lauderdale Police Department. I would like to speak to a member of your management team."

In a short while they were sitting in a conference room with a senior executive who conveyed the sympathies of the grieving staff and extended their willingness to cooperate in the investigation. Salter asked if he could spend the morning talking to those who worked most closely with Emily Patrick. The executive took them to the webcasting department made up of several women and their female supervisor. They learned that Emily's cubicle was next to the desk of a young woman named Monica who knew her best and was considered a close friend. They took Monica to the conference room and sat at a long table in front of a large blank screen used for video meetings with other company locations.

"Don't be nervous," Ramos said. "We just want to know everything we can about what Emily was like. Anything that might help with our investigation."

"I'll help in any way I can," Monica said. "I'm still heartbroken over this."

Ramos nodded. "I know. It's so hard. First, what can you tell us about her? What was she like?"

"Oh, the nicest person you would ever meet. She was a good friend. Sometimes, we did things together on weekends."

"Like what?"

"We would go to craft shows sometimes. We both liked that sort of thing."

"Go ahead—tell us anything that comes to mind. And if there is anything at all that you think might help us, please let us know."

"Hmm—she liked doing videos on YouTube although she didn't talk about it much. I think I was one of the few people here that knew. She was obsessed with anything Japanese. She loved anime and cosplay and even went to Japan."

"She had gone recently. Can you describe what she was like before and after the trip."

"Huge difference. She was so excited before her trip, but when she got back she was a different person. She was acting strange—almost couldn't do her job. I kept having to help her. I hate to say it, but it was almost as if she was mentally ill when she returned from Japan. She would say things about creatures in her ears and how she needed to draw Chinese lions for protection."

"Protection from what?" Ramos asked.

"I don't know. But I thought it might be jetlag. Maybe her body never adapted to the time change. Maybe she couldn't sleep at night."

"Do you know of any reason why someone would want to hurt Emily?"

"No. She was a really nice person."

"Were there any office conflicts involving Emily that you had ever noticed? Was anyone upset at her?"

"No."

"Were there any guys here at work interested in her?"

"I'm sure that none of the guys minded seeing her. As they say, she was easy on the eyes. Sometimes guys would show up just to talk to her. I knew they were more interested in her than me."

"Do you know if any of those guys might have had psychological issues?"

"Not really. They all seem normal."

Salter leaned forward. "Did Emily lock her phone? he asked.

"Uh, I don't know—I never noticed."

"Did she leave her phone unattended—leave it out where someone could tamper with it, say, when she would go to the restroom?"

"I don't remember. I think she left it on her desk sometimes."

Salter tensed his brow. "Did anyone ever use it besides her?"

"The only person that ever touched her phone was Charles, one of the net-ops guys. He would troubleshoot her phone sometimes for her if she was having problems."

"Can you take us to see him?"

"Sure—but he's not the kind of person—uh—you know what I mean?"

"We know what you mean."

Monica took Salter and Ramos to a cavernous area in the back of the building. It had once been used to as newsroom for financial breaking stories to stream in the early days of the internet. The executives at NXP thought that by releasing stock trading news fifteen minutes before most media outlets at the top of the hour, they would give their subscribers an advantage worth paying premium monthly fees. When the U.S. Securities and Exchange Commission issued the Regulation Fair Disclosure, requiring that all publicly traded companies disclose information to all investors at the same time, NXP had no other choice than to close its financial news division. The large newsroom was converted mostly to a storage area, and beyond the piles of old servers and computer equipment were the cubicles belonging to the net-ops team.

Monica opened one of the glass soundproof doors to the loud machine gun noise of a video game. Salter nodded and indicated that he would take it from there, entering the room with Ramos in search of Charles. They passed a set of drums, guitars, amplifiers, a mountain of CRT monitors and other obsolete relics. The only person in the room was a man in his thirties with long blonde hair furiously blasting away with his game controls. Salter and Ramos walked up to him and stood behind him.

"Excuse me!" Salter shouted. "Excuse me!"

Salter tapped his shoulder. The man turned around.

"Could you please turn that down?"

"Oh—sorry," he said while pausing the game.

"We're detectives with the Fort Lauderdale Police Department. Are you Charles?"

"Yeah—that's me."

"We were wondering if we could talk to you about Emily Patrick," Salter said. "Do you have a moment to talk to us?"

"Yeah—it's terrible what happened to Emily. Is there anything I can help you with?"

"You mind if we sit down? You're here alone?"

Salter and Ramos rolled two office chairs close to where Charles had been playing the game in front of a sixty inch screen.

"I'm the only one here right now," Charles said.

"Would you like to talk here or go into the conference room?"

"This is fine," he said.

"What exactly do you do here?" Salter asked.

"I maintain the company network and all the computers."

"You have time to play video games?"

"They pay me shit and make me work long hours. So it's sort of a fringe benefit. I can play games and they let my band practice here after work hours. But, sometimes I'm very busy. This is one of our down times."

"We understand that you would sometimes help Emily Patrick troubleshoot her phone problems. Did you ever install any software on her phone?"

"Uh—the last thing I installed on her phone was an app to control a camera that I gave her."

"A Sony Action Cam?"

"Yes, that's the one. All I really did was download the software from the Android App store."

"Why did you give her that camera?"

"She needed a camera for her YouTube videos—something better than her phone camera."

"And why an Action Cam?"

"I wasn't using it. I bought it do a video for our band. We mounted it on a bicycle handle bar and got some cool effects riding around."

"Were you close to Emily?" Ramos asked.

"I never saw her outside of work," Charles said. "But I helped her a lot with technical stuff—but only at work."

"Do you know anything about surveillance software?" Salter asked.

"Not really."

"Malware—Spyware?"

"Well, I have to know about that stuff. Computers get infected and I have to remove viruses all the time. Do you think I put something on Emily's phone—besides the camera app?"

Salter stretched his neck by tilting and rotating his head. "We're not saying you did anything. But please try to help us understand. How would surveillance software get on her phone?"

"I don't know."

"Had you ever dated Emily in the past?" Ramos asked.

"I told you, I didn't know her outside of work."

"Do you believe that Emily was attracted to you or had any kind of interest in you?"

"No."

"Do you have a history of being rejected by women?"

"Doesn't every guy?"

"Do you have a problem communicating with women?"

"Not really."

"Would you consider yourself socially awkward—any low self-esteem?"

"No and no."

"Do you have any unusual pets?"

"No."

"Do you have friends?"

"Yes, my bandmates and all the people I've met over the years. I'm I a suspect?"

Salter made a slight sigh. "To tell you truth, you don't fit the profile, but you're the only one that we know of that had possession of Emily's phone. Someone was cyberstalking her and then that someone killed her and removed the spyware from her phone. Is there anything you can tell us to help solve this murder?"

"Look—I'll take a polygraph, give you DNA—anything you want. But please don't think I had anything to do with this."

"We appreciate the offer," Salter said. "If we were to look at the web browsing history on your computer, would we find porn related to violence against women?"

"No."

"Hmm," Salter sighed with discouragement. "This is frustrating. Our search has led us to you, but you seem like a dead end. How are we going to find our killer? Is there anything at all you can tell us?"

"I'm sorry," Charles said. "I wish I could help."

"Just curious," Ramos said. "Did you notice Emily acting strange when she returned from Japan?"

"Yeah—she was acting kind of strange."

"How so?"

"It was like she was sad or something. She kept cupping her ears. Why was she like that?"

"We're not entirely sure."

"And she did say that she had been having problems with her phone. She wanted me to look at it, but I was swamped with work at the time. I doubt I would have found any spyware on her phone. Those things become invisible. The person that installs it doesn't want anyone to know it's there."

"You don't think you would have found it—a net-ops person?"

"Think about it—I'm certified to service PC's and conventional network hardware. I would need a whole new skillset to be an expert on mobile devices. I know a little, but not a lot. And as little as they pay me, why would I want to go through additional certification programs."

"I see your point."

"But as far as phone cyber stalking, a lot of parents are doing it because they're worried about what their kids are doing. You install the spyware and it makes full logs of every text message. Everything the kid deletes, the parent can still see. They can use the GPS to always know where their kids are."

"And what if the person is professional person like you, or a programmer?"

"The sky is the limit. They can make a phone turn on when it's off. Operate the microphone and video—whatever they can imagine, they can probably do."

"That's kind of scary," Ramos said.

"That's the world we live in."

Salter smacked his lips. "You've been telling us the truth the entire time, haven't you?"

"I really don't know anything," Charles said.

"Well, wish us luck. I think we need it. Please don't discuss our conversation with anyone."

Salter noticed a paper gun range target hanging on the wall in another cubicle. The black silhouette with circles labeled 7, 8, 9, was filled with bullet holes.

"Who sits there?" Salter asked.

"Ulysses Garcia."

"He's a net-ops person like you?"

"Oh, he can do a lot more than me. He used to be on the software development team."

"He's not here today?"

"No. He took a personal day."

"We should go to his home," Salter told Ramos.

"We can't, we've got a meeting with the victim's family tonight," she said.

# CHAPTER SIXTEEN

That evening Emily Patrick's family came to the police department to ask questions about the investigation. In a meeting room cluttered with boxes containing case files, Mr. and Mrs. Patrick sat with their son Eliot, a man with a tense demeanor. Salter was the last to walk into the room as Rob and Hector assured the family that they were doing everything they could to bring justice to Emily's untimely death. Kim Ramos listened carefully, paying special attention to Eliot's habit of twitching his lips as if experiencing physical discomfort.

"Thank you for coming," Salter said as he sat down. "I'm Detective Ryan Salter. I head this homicide unit. I just want to say that I'm profoundly sorry for you loss. We've made solving this crime our top priority. We're doing everything we possibly can. I'm sure you have a lot of questions. We also have a few questions. How should we do this? Should we ask the questions first or save them for later?"

"We only have a few questions," Mr. Patrick meekly said.

"Okay. You want to go first?"

"Yes," said Mr. Patrick. "Your detective just mentioned that you don't have a suspect. Is this true?"

"We have people of interest," Salter said. "We won't consider them suspects until we have reason to believe they're guilty. We've actually been pretty busy questioning people that appeared to be close enough to Emily to warrant suspicion. We'll follow the trail to see where it leads."

Mrs. Patrick sighed and wiped her teary eyes. "Do you think you'll find who did this? Do you know why anyone would do this?"

"We're doing everything we can," Salter said. "Detective Ramos and I haven't slept since Emily was found. As far as motive, we don't have one yet. I'm not sure you would want to hear every detail, because these things can be disturbing. Besides, a grieving family shouldn't have to listen to all this. Give yourselves a few days to recover from the shock. If you really need to know, I'll tell you everything, but I don't recommend it. Not yet. Give yourselves at least a few days to deal with this tragedy. If things go right, we'll find out who did this and the details of how we caught him won't matter so much anymore."

"Uh-uh—Florida still has the-the death penalty, right?" Eliot stuttered.

"Yes," Ramos quietly nodded.

"So you have evidence that you can use in court?" Mr. Patrick asked.

"We have some evidence," Slater said. "But it's too early to tell how everything is going to play out and how a legal case will be made."

"Tell us honestly, does this look like the kind of case that has a good chance of being solved?"

Salter nodded. "We were fortunate enough to find Emily's phone. People store so much information on their phones that we made this case our top priority because it seems likely to us that we'll be able to figure something of what happened. Emily left a digital footprint for us. We know quite a bit about her from her internet usage and the things she did and places she went. We've logged quite a bit of information about her interests and all sorts of things that have helped us better understand her. We're really trying hard."

"Thank you, detective," Mrs. Patrick said.

"You said you had some questions for us," Mr. Patrick said.

"Yes," Detective Ostroff said. "Do you ever remember Emily being harassed by anyone online—or offline for that matter?"

"No," said Mrs. Patrick.

Eliot and Mr. Patrick shook their heads.

"Ever have a jealous boyfriend," Ramos asked.

Mrs. Patrick crinkled her forehead. "Her last boyfriend that she introduced us to seemed like a nice young man. It didn't last that long, and I don't think they ever saw each other again. I'm sure there were more young men that we didn't know about. Lots of boys were dying to go out with her."

"Nobody was good enough for my sister," Eliot said. "It's true. She was special."

Ramos gave Eliot as sad smile. "You knew your sister well."

"She'll never be forgotten," Eliot said. "She *was* impermanence. We—what are we? We're just people. But she—she was more. You might say she was a kind of high priestess—priestess of gardens and mysteries, light and darkness. We—mere humans—don't have ears to hear, nor sight, not even a voice. We don't have any of those things. We think we do, but they're only things we dream up because we wished we were like Emily. I know I must sound overly dramatic. I'm not trying to be a poet. I don't usually talk like this. But I was her brother. I'm hurting. What is left but a gaping wound? She was plucked away and what are we to do without her? There is nothing left but absence. Not only is our light gone, there is also no darkness. She was a little like me, too sensitive for this world. But somehow, through her magnificence and splendor, she conquered a fear and pain that no one in this world can even imagine. She was a raw nerve that could scream with agony—and then one day she became numb. And in this numbness, she managed to keep her soul and find happiness. She had magical powers, you know-"

"Eliot," Mrs. Patrick whispered as if pleading for mercy.

"Yes—yes. She was magical. She could leave her body at night and-"

"This is not the time for this," Mr. Patrick said.

"It's okay," Salter said. "If you don't mind, I would like to hear this."

Mr. Patrick shrugged.

"At first she thought they were dreams," Eliot continued. "As a little girl she was frightened of her out of body experiences, but eventually she surrendered to them. Only a very sensitive person can find the exact threshold between consciousness and unconsciousness and vibrate to another energy frequency. While the rest of us were living ordinary lives, who knows what adventures she was experiencing."

"How do you know this?" Ramos asked.

"She told me."

"Did you always believe her?"

"Yes, I believed her."

"Did she keep this a secret?"

"Yes—only a few people knew."

"And can you think of any possible way these secrets might be related to someone trying to kill her?"

"Possibly," Eliot nodded. "Since she was mysterious, someone must have been afraid of her. Anything that is dark and unknowable represents a threat to those whose lives are based on fear. FDR said that the only thing we have to fear is fear itself, but it seems those words fell on deaf ears. The bible says that perfect love casts out all fear, but those words have also fallen on deaf ears. It is fear that causes us to be suspicious of other people—causes us to hate. It is fear that causes one country to attack another. It is fear that turns the devout and religious into self-righteous, angry, condemning hypocrites. It is fear that causes the police to use lethal force on unarmed citizens. It is the fear of mystery, secrets and unknowable things that caused someone to kill my sister. It is those who declare themselves to be good that are often evil. It is those we fear as evil that are often like the Samaritan—loving and generous. Good is sometimes evil and evil is sometimes good. But fear makes us all evil. And Emily—Emily was fearless and blameless. She was perfect and—because there is evil in the world—they took my Emily away. "

"Hmm—you're quite a brother," Ramos said. "You say such kind things about Emily."

"The world needs to know how wonderful my sister was."

"Maybe her videos will stay up on YouTube."

"You better believe they will. I'm going to figure out a way to save them and then upload them to every video sharing website in existence. I hope she can hear me. I hope she knows how much I love her."

Ramos saw tear streaming down Eliot's face and let out a sad breath. "I think she does."

Salter pressed his fist against his chin and looked sadly at Eliot. "As soon as we're done with her laptop, you can have it. All her videos are on the hard drive."

...

After meeting with Emily's parents, Sergeant Salter went home for the evening. He took a shower and then went into the kitchen and poured himself a bowl of cereal. He placed his phone besides the box of Corn Flakes and scrolled through notifications. Photos of his baby nephews made him smile briefly. Too tired to check the rest of his social media newsfeed, he pushed the phone away and let the screen go black. He stared at a picture of his sister and her family on the wall. He thought of the kind of brother he was to her—if he would ever have such heartfelt sentiments for his sister as Eliot had.

Salter went to bed but couldn't sleep. His mind was active with thoughts about the investigation. Charles was telling the truth. Charles answered every question exactly the way he should have. No, Charles is not a sociopath. He was telling the truth. The guy in the other cubicle—the guy with the gun range target—could he have installed the spyware on the phone when Charles was away from his desk? Could he be the killer? If he's the guy, he could have shot her, but he strangled her instead. He's sneaky. He didn't want to leave behind any ballistics evidence. How would he respond to questions? What would an investigation of him reveal?

Salter sprang up in bed, frustrated that his overactive mind was keeping him from the sleep he desperately needed. He went back to the kitchen, picked up the phone and selected the name Margo from his contacts. She arrived within the hour, throwing a purse on the sofa and pecking Ryan Salter on the lips.

"I just want you know that I haven't slept in two days," he said.

"That's okay," she said.

They went to his bedroom.

"I'm so tired," he said.

"Can't sleep, huh?" she asked.

"No."

"Need to unwind?"

"That's what I was hoping for."

Margo cupped his face with her hands and planted tiny kisses on him. Ryan leaned back in bed and closed his eyes.

"Aren't you glad you found me on Craigslist?"

"I already put some money in your PayPal."

"Thanks."

She held him and watched his eyes slowly close as he drifted off. He awoke at five in the morning to find Margo with him under the covers.

"How'd you sleep?" she asked.

"Not bad."

"You're my only client-you know."

"Oh really," he said with a note of sarcasm.

"It's true. I always screened all my dates. But now there's just you. I like you."

"I like you too."

"So when are you going to settle down?"

"Oh, I don't want to do that," he sighed.

"Why not?"

"It never works out."

"Sometimes it does."

"Men and women are completely incompatible. It's like they're two totally different species. God must have thought it was funny, creating us like this. And personally, I just can't take all the drama."

"What drama?"

"The moods. I work a lot of hours. I get so tired. I can't imagine dealing with moodiness after a long day, or two day shift."

"You can't deal with even a little moodiness? she asked.

"Noooo," he feigned sadness.

"But you're going to die of loneliness."

He sighed. "So be it."

"Isn't there anyone that you think you might get along with?"

"My partner is cute as hell, but she's married—and probably a little too young for me."

"That's why you don't need anyone. You've got your partner."

"She's just a partner."

"She makes you happy."

"Maybe a little."

"Or maybe you're just missing the falling in love gene."

"You know what's strange?"

"What?"

"I think I'm falling in love with another dead person."

"Homicide victim?"

"Yes."

"That's so sad."

"She seemed so perfect. God, I want to catch her killer."

"I can imagine."

"What do you normally do for a living?"

"I'm an accountant."

"I thought you were going to say that you were a therapist."

"I'd make a good therapist."

"Yes, you would."

"When do you have to be ready for work?"

"Soon."

Salter went to use the bathroom. After flushing the toilet, he walked out scratching the stubble on his face. "What kind of name is Ulysses?"

"Who's that?" Margo asked.

"A person of interest in a case I'm working on."

"Like Ulysses Grant, the president?"

"Yeah—who would name their child that?"

"I don't know. Are you okay?"

"Frustrated—I tried to be optimistic for the victim's family last night. I made it seem like there was a chance of catching the guy. I didn't tell them that we had no physical evidence or a motive. If this Ulysses character didn't do it, I'm not sure where our investigation goes after that."

# CHAPTER SEVENTEEN

## Days before the Murder

Four months after the accident, Ulysses' leg had healed. He could now sit in front of his computer at work without dreading the next urge to go to the restroom or employee lounge. Work had been slow for a while and he had time to read and watch videos online. On days when his coworker, Charles, wasn't at work, Ulysses would spend most of the day watching Emily Patrick's YouTube channel. He had become convinced that she was reading his thoughts. Because she was such a threat to him, he tried to find out as much as he could about her. During one of her ASMR role plays, he paused the video to stare at her Tōhoku earthquake and tsunami relief poster on her wall. The prominent number eleven in the date filled him with trepidation.

He attempted to sooth his anxiety by watching the new Nestor Turk channel, created to quench public demand for something greater than a podcast. Turk's talking head appeared, acknowledging the viewer with a knowing look:

The Illuminati—whatever you want to call them—they go by many names. They're Satan's hands on earth. They're here to do the devil's work on this planet. And then there are us, people of God—here to do God's work. Once you understand this concept, you will see it everywhere. Everywhere you look, you'll see the symbols, the secret codes and evidence for the creation of a new world order. We've discussed all these things in detail. The symbols are everywhere and they're as plain as day. Let's just be reasonable, everyone. Something is definitely going on. And, as we know, the illuminati are Satanists. So when you watch the Super Bowl or the awards shows and the commercials, you'll see all these satanic symbols. All you need to do is see that all these things are connected. The Satanists, who call themselves mystics—they contact interdimensional beings. The aliens—the demons—high level masons. It is written, there shall arise false Christs and false prophets, and shall show great signs. So, as a faithful and obedient person of God, you should be aware that these signs are everywhere. I'm here to inform you. In Numerology, the number eleven represents sin and transgression. Ten is the perfect number. Eleven tries to be better than ten, like Lucifer trying to surpass God. People who are creative and think of themselves as visionaries or are simply attracted to the unknown and open to experience—these people are drawn to the number eleven. The things of God, which are awesome and splendid, are simply not enough for the number eleven people. They think they're too intelligent and easily bored with the ordinary. They want darkness and mystery—the supernatural. They are instruments of Satan, bringing a demonic system to earth. They call it the higher consciousness movement. Whenever you hear these people talking about love and higher consciousness, don't believe any of it. It all has to do with the age of the antichrist—the time we are living in now. Have you ever awoken in the middle of the night to see that the time is 1:11? There is definitely something going on, my friends. 111 times the six days of creation is 666. I just have to point this out, folks. This is serious stuff. Keep your eyes on the skies. The devil is the prince of the air. Watch out for the symbols and the number eleven people…

Ulysses selected the remote viewer program from his system files and navigated through the network to Emily Patrick's computer. All the company computers had the remote software installed so that the network administrators could update security software, fix something or, if necessary, investigate an employee's productivity. Without Emily knowing, Ulysses checked her browsing history to see what websites she had been navigating to. She had done numerous Google searches for Chinese foo dogs. They seemed grotesque to him, the very depiction of evil.

Then he scoured her personal photos, hoping to find a folder of more revealing pictures, but there was nothing provocative. He wrote down her name on a small piece of paper and counted the number of letters in it. Emily Patrick had twelve letters, not eleven. Despite this, he still considered her to be a number eleven type of person. Everyone knew about her outings with Monica to the arts and craft shows. And then there was her ASMR channel, undeniably an interest in something unusual and counter to what would be considered normal. It was obvious to him that she was a person of creativity and open to experience. This susceptibility to step into the unfamiliar and possibly dark unknown realms distressed him.

After he was satisfied that he had combed through every bit of her personal information stored on her work computer, he decided to explore her phone. He had installed spyware on it when Emily had left it with Charles for maintenance. As soon as Charles had walked out of the room, Ulysses connected a cable to it and transferred the software. Even before her trip to Japan, he had been monitoring her texts and emails for a while, but now that he felt threatened and convinced of her status as an eleven, he needed to understand, categorize and label every facet of her life so that he could feel safe from her.

He went through her photo gallery until he found a more recent picture of her in shorts. He took a deep breath and slowly let it out, savoring the contours of her legs. They looked soft and silky to him, shapely with the thigh gap his wife obsessed about. Unable to find any more photos like this, he became frustrated and turned to his computer. Browsing in stealth mode, he searched for black models. Then he searched for sexy black models. Then he searched for naked black models.

His breathing became heavy and clicked off on the browser window to stop the stream of tantalizing images. He wiped his clammy face and huffed in anger. *She made me do this*, he said to himself. He picked up the piece of paper that he had written her name on and looked at it again, trying to form an anagram. After a few minutes he thought of the words karmic type li. *Who was Li? Kung Fu master Li? —From a graphic novel or video game? —Or could it be the roman numbers—LI—51.*

*Emily Patrick—karmic type Li. Once a person understands the truth about the new world order, he should be able to see the symbols everywhere*, he remembered Turk's words. He researched this online and within a few minutes he had found a connection between the Li family of China and the Rockefellers and Rothschilds. A webpage stated that Japan and China would both play significant roles in the new world order. The Li family, which had founded the Tang dynasty, controlled a secret society called the Triads. The Triads were part of a satanic hierarchy, according to information he gathered on the Internet, which meant that the Li family were members of the illuminati. Oh my God, Ulysses gasped.

More search engine results led Ulysses to articles about the Triads and their organized crime activities worldwide as well as their animal sacrifice initiation rituals and their presence in most countries with a significant Chinese population. He now saw the Chinese foo dogs as something more than just demonic symbols; they were proof of Emily's allegiance to the Li family. But what about Japan? Emily went to Japan. What was the Chinese and Japanese connection?

Eventually, Ulysses had worked out an elaborate conspiracy between the Bank of Japan and the Chinese secret societies to pave the way for the new world order. The two countries seemed to be moving toward one currency; at least this was his suspicion. They would be able to convert between yuan and yen without switching to dollars first. Despite the appearance that the two countries were not getting along, the opposite seemed to be true.

Even with his monitoring of Emily, he had not been able to determine what she had actually done in Japan. It seemed to him that she was profoundly involved in a secret plot to usher in the age of the antichrist. Karmic type Li was like a member of a sleeper cell, waiting for an awakening. Her presence at a technology company and her friendship with Charles suggested a horde of nefarious possibilities.

Ulysses practically trembled with a sense of purpose. He had been divinely ordained to battle the forces of darkness, uncovering secret enemy stratagem. Who else, but him, could have fit all the pieces together so perfectly? He thought about these things some more as he looked at a photo of Emily, moving his fingers apart on the touchscreen to zoom in on her face. He traced the outline of her lips.

*The devil is supposed to be beautiful. Lucifer was an angel of light. Karmic type Li is one of his demons—so beautiful. What a shame, to waste one's life in service of the evil one. Beauty means nothing. It is temporary. God is eternal. He will triumph. I will help him. The beauty of Japan, the beauty of Karma type Li. What does it matter? There will be a new heaven and a new earth. The old earth will pass away. Beauty is a lie from hell. It is an illusion. The luminous angel will come and try to deceive everyone with knowledge and happiness and peace. These are simply attempts to seduce us. I must admit that Karmic type Li is tempting me, but even the son of man was tempted when he was forty days in the wilderness. If I am to destroy her, I must accept that the temptations will not cease.*

Ulysses activated the surveillance software on his phone and selected Emily's profile. Her GPS showed that she was at the Miami Beach Convention Center. He turned on her microphone and listened to the din of the many people inside the building. The front facing and rear facing cameras didn't provide any images.

Later, he found and read the emails between Simeon Suslov and Emily and decided that he wanted to carefully monitor her activities that evening. Ulysses told Melanie that he was going to the gun range, but instead of shooting targets, he sat in his car with his phone plugged into the cigarette lighter socket, listening to the gathering of The Hermetic Order of the Mystic Koyosha. When he had determined that it was a secret society with a member of the Japanese aristocracy present, he started his engine and made his way to the Jafet mansion, the location that Emily's GPS indicated.

He parked not far from the entrance to the community and waited for Emily's car to leave. Toshi and Emily's conversation about being great warriors and traveling through different dimensions together made his plan to confront Emily seem even more urgent and necessary. When he saw her car pass the security gate he tailed her for several miles until she stopped at a red light and he pulled up alongside of her. He gave the horn a slight honk and Emily turned to look in his direction. When he lowered the passenger side window, she could see that it was him.

"Emily—what a coincidence!"

"Oh, hi Ulysses!"

"Hey, I know that you like Japanese things. Did you know that there was a small shrine at the park we're about to pass?"

"What—no way!"

"Follow me—I'll show you."

"You're kidding, right? How could I live here all my life and not know about that?"

"I'm serious, follow me!"

"Okay—but I'll believe it when I see it."

When the light turned green, Ulysses' car pulled ahead and the two drove for about a quarter of a mile until reaching the entrance to the park. Emily was afraid of leaving her small backpack in the car unattended and took it with her. She followed him past a nature trail into a clearing.

"There's even a torii gate in front of the Shinto shrine," Ulysses said.

"You've got to be making this up," Emily laughed.

"No, I'm not making this up."

"God, I'm so tired. I can't believe that after all the gazillions of temples and shrines I saw in Japan, I can't pass up seeing this."

Ulysses reached into his pocket and quietly snapped on latex gloves. Emily thought she heard the sound of rubber bands and started to turn. He moved behind her and then swung his fist as hard as he could, striking the back of her head, behind the ear. Emily collapsed unconscious. Then he strangled her. After he had removed all her clothes, he stared at her for a while.

*I had to do this quickly, before she started reading my thoughts again. I outwitted her! I lured Karmic type Li with the prospect of a shrine to a false god. The hands of Satan on this earth, she cannot fulfill whatever purpose she was given. Lucifer, beautiful angel of light, I have destroyed one of your demons. All this dark beauty, I absorb it, I take it all in. I am righteous. I am pious. I did not violate her. I did not act on my lust. A soldier in God's army will eventually come face to face with temptation. However, I have overcome.*

He reached into her backpack and pulled out her sketchbook. The drawings of lion-dogs illuminated by an almost full moon repulsed him as he turned several of the pages. Each foo dog face seemed to look back at him in anger, expressing outrage for the slaying. He tore the pages out and created a circle around her, hoping to separate Emily and all her dark talismans from the rest of the world. He rummaged through her purse and found her phone. He removed the spyware and threw it also within the circle.

He now felt a strange mixture of peace and dark satisfaction—emotionally and physically drained by the violence he had committed. The fear of Emily had been replaced by the gratification of serving the Lord against the forces of Satan. He could still feel her warm neck in his ferocious grip. When he got back to his car and removed the gloves, his hands felt strangely cold and tingly.

*Karmic type Li—it is the heathen that believe in karma. She is no longer a threat to anyone. Besides, I never liked pretty girls anyway. They always rejected me.*

. . .

When he got home, he turned his phone on. He hadn't wanted any digital record of his location that evening. There were, of course, cameras on every traffic light. They would have proven that he was in the area of the crime, but would the investigation ever come to that? Where would they think to look? It would be the proverbial needle in a haystack. And if they actually had him on video, what would it prove? It was all circumstantial evidence. But what if the police were clever enough to find the traffic cam evidence? Would he reveal something in an interrogation to incriminate himself? He would have to lawyer up. The relentless questioning would probably cause him to say something that needed to be hidden. However, Ulysses felt fairly certain that there was nothing to tie him to Emily. Would a homicide investigator even work with a traffic investigator? What if there were new types of software designed to look for a particular driver somewhere in the city? But why would anyone think to run his license plate numbers through a database? He hadn't told anyone about his war against the illuminati. No detective could possibly know what's going on. He sat in his car and pondered these things for a while before going inside his home.

He was about to put the key in the door when another thought occurred to him. What if his wife asked him about the gun range? He couldn't tell her that he had actually done any shooting. It would be too easy for police to catch him in a lie that way. He couldn't tell them that he spent most of the evening in his car. Even if he said that he had found an interesting program on the satellite radio and decided to sit and listen to it, the traffic cams proved otherwise. Everything kept coming back to the video cameras at every intersection. The simplest thing, he concluded, was to stick to one story. He went to the gun range with the intention of shooting, but decided that he needed time to think about his life, so he drove around the city reflecting on his career and future. If his car was caught on camera next to Emily's car at an intersection, it could just be explained as a coincidence.

That night, he was awoken from his sleep by a loud explosion in his head.

"Did you hear that?" he asked.

"Huh?"

"Did you hear that?"

"No, I didn't hear anything."

"It was like a loud blast. Like someone fired a gun and blew out my brains. Actually, it was almost like sword striking my skull so hard that it shattered into a million pieces. The Native Americans used to do that with tomahawks. One swing and the head would explode like a watermelon."

"It was a bad dream," she said.

"It was so loud."

"Are you taking any medications?"

"No. I stopped taking the hypertension pills."

"Okay, go back to sleep."

"Could it be?"

"Could what be?"

"That they want revenge."

"Who—Revenge for what?"

"Nothing…"

The next day, Ulysses went to work, determined to find out more about the Li family, the Bank of Japan and the Mystic Koyosha so he could begin launching cyber-attacks. He was distracted by new videos suggested to him by YouTube based on his past viewing preferences. According to one person, the Large Hadron Collider was an attempt to summon the great beast from the depths of the earth or another dimension. As he watched the man explaining how 666 had been hidden in the CERN logo, a disturbing realization came to him: Emily was not the only one who could listen to his thoughts. He felt a presence in the room, probing his head.

"Just to let you know, I'm taking a personal day tomorrow," Ulysses said.

"Okay," Charles replied. "Hey, did you hear the news?"

"No—what?"

"Emily Patrick died last night."

# CHAPTER EIGHTEEN

"Pastor Bill is not a true believer!" Ulysses shouted back.

"What is wrong with you?" Melanie responded.

"Listen to me—Bill doesn't have the fire of God. He's lukewarm. All this talk about community and loving one another is for sissies! Anyone who's read the bible should realize the wrath coming upon us. I even have reason to believe that he is a freethinker. Freethinkers are doing the work of Satan."

"You know what your problem is?"

"What—what's my problem?"

"You have the mind of a fourteen year old. Grow up!"

"Screw you!"

"There's a reason you take everything so seriously—it's because of your huge ego! Who do you think you are? Who are you to judge a man that spends most of his time helping people—a man that is making next to nothing just to see if he can make a difference in the community? He doesn't get any of the attention that the senior pastor gets when he's delivering his sermons. He's just a nice, quiet, humble man—someone who has to put up with criticism every day. And you—you sound like you're out of your mind half the time. With such arrogance, I really don't know what you're capable of anymore."

"How do you know Bill so well? Are you sleeping with him?"

"You're pathetic."

"You are—aren't you?"

"There's something really wrong with you."

"You won't answer my question. That means you are sleeping with him."

"I am not sleeping with him!"

"All right, that's all I needed to hear. But you better always tell me the truth. I know a lot more than you realize."

Melanie rolled her eyes. "What is that supposed to mean?"

"You say that I take everything too seriously, but you don't take anything serious. You're not careful. You need to be extremely careful."

"Careful with what?"

"Everything! Did you know that when the feds gave the Branch Davidians cartons of milk for the children, they put listening devices inside of them?"

"Why are you bringing up Waco? You know, you're starting to remind me a little of David Koresh."

"I'm just saying that everything I know, I need to keep inside my head because people might be listening."

"Yules—you need to see a psychologist."

"No, I don't, but you need to wake up and see that the world is evil and that we're in great danger."

"Please, I'm begging you. Get some counseling."

"I hate your dismissive attitude," Ulysses turned red with anger. "I'm crazy, because I see things you can't? A prophet is never honored in his hometown."

"You're a prophet now-"

"I have been chosen."

Melanie made a languid motion with her head. "This all started after your traffic accident. You were saying all kinds of crazy shit as the anesthesia was wearing off. Did the hallucinations ever stop? Did they?"

"The things I see are real."

"You see yourself as some great anointed one. Pastor Bill, the most humble man we know, is a threat to you. That's why you despise him."

"You don't realize who you're speaking to," Ulysses squinted.

"Who are you, Ulysses?"

"You mentioned David Koresh. He called himself the final prophet. Maybe I'm the one who is the final prophet."

"I'm glad you think so highly of yourself."

There was a knock on the door.

"I'll get it," Ulysses said.

When he opened the door, Salter and Ramos were standing outside.

"Mr. Garcia?" Ramos said.

"Uh—I don't have to talk to you," Ulysses said almost in a whisper.

"Can we please come in for a moment?" Salter lifted his police ID.

"I'm not required to allow you inside my home. It is my constitutional right."

Salter sighed. "Please talk to us for just a moment."

Ulysses shook his head.

"Can we ask you why you weren't at work yesterday?"

"No, you cannot."

"How did you get that bruise on your knuckle?"

"I'm closing the door now. I don't have to talk to you."

Ulysses slammed the door. Salter and Ramos exchanged glances and went back to the car.

"I'm really liking this guy for the crime," Salter said. "How do we connect him?"

Ramos shrugged. "Check his computer at work—computer at home-"

"This guy is a software engineer and a network administrator. I bet he knows how to cover his tracks. But suppose we find that he was cyberstalking our victim. Will it be enough to prove he killed her?"

"He might crack under interrogation."

"I bet he's rehearsing answers as we speak. Now that he knows we're on to him, I wonder what he's up to."

"I sure wish we had enough to get search warrants and arrest him."

"We can't do anything. I think I saw his wife and a small child. I wonder if they're safe for the night. What if he slaughters his family tonight? I'll never be able to live with myself."

"There's nothing we can do?"

"Not much. Wait—I thought of something. I know a cop who used to work for the U.S. Dept. of Health and Human Resources. If there's a tomorrow, I have a plan…"

…

The following morning, just as Ulysses was logging on to the network at NXP Webcasting, a man with a striking resemblance to William Shatner walked into the Net-Ops room.

"Are you Ulysses Garcia?" he asked.

"Uh—yes. I am he."

"My name is Barry Conomikes. I'm an agent for the U.S. Dept. of Health and Human Resources. I will be going over your company's HIPAA policies with you and asking you some questions."

"Nobody told me about this," Ulysses said with a note of displeasure.

"It's an unannounced visit. We do this all the time to make sure that people's personal information is protected."

"What do you want to know?"

Barry Conomikes pulled up a chair, slowly rolled up his sleeves, and gave Ulysses a menacing look.

"Everything—I want to know everything. Let's start with you giving me an approximation of how many patients' personal information is stored on your servers. How many of your clients are healthcare recipients?"

"It's hard to say," Ulysses sighed. "We do many corporate webcasts. Some are medical companies. The users fill out online registration forms so they can view the event."

"Hard to say?" Conomikes lifted his eyebrows. "There are at least fifty different policies that need to be in place and you need to be aware of them. You're the senior network administrator. The hammer is going to come down hard on you."

"Look I-"

"Are you aware of the severe penalties for HIPAA violations? Do you have any idea what happens if there is no protection plan in place? Do you know what happens when there is misuse and disclosures of personal information? Do you know what happens if you don't exercise reasonable diligence in acquainting yourself with HIPAA policies? There can be a fifty thousand dollar civil penalty with up to 1.5 million dollars annually. If we find that you knowingly accessed a person's personal information, you could go to prison for up to ten years!"

"Look—I-"

"Which is fine with me. I make my money from all the fines that corporations have to pay."

"Isn't that a conflict of interest?"

"What did you say?"

"You have an incentive to trump up-"

"You better not piss me off!"

"Uh—I-"

"We receive thousands of complaints of HIPAA violations. A lot of those are referred to the US Department of Justice. People go to prison all the time, not just when there's a major breach and someone hacks into a company's computers and steals credit card numbers. I hope you understand the gravity of this. You must comply with the rules concerning administrative safeguards. You must adopt a set of privacy procedures. There must be a contingency plan in place for responding to security breaches. If there were a security breach, how long would you wait before disclosing and announcing the incident to the public?"

"Uh-"

"Do you understand what I am asking?"

"Look—uh—you should really talk to the CTO."

"I'm talking to you!"

"I don't appreciate you speaking to me in that tone," Ulysses turned his face away.

"You don't like my tone? Tell me, are you emotionally stable? Did you know that most of computer hacking and damage done to networks are by disgruntled former employees? Have you written time bomb code into the company's computers in the event of your termination?"

"Time bomb code?"

"Yes, you're a programmer. You are more than capable of writing a few lines of code that the other software engineers won't notice—something to take down the whole system as revenge for a firing. Or perhaps you have to enter a number once a month to prevent the time bomb from going off."

"No—haven't snuck any code into our systems."

"How do we know that? I get the impression that you're a loafer or maybe someone that is incompetent at their job. People with no talent, skills or imagination are often very destructive. You might even have a predisposition for causing harm. But as far as I can see, there is no professionalism in your work ethic. Why aren't all the HIPAA policies your most important priority? Is that a password written down on a post-it note? Don't you realize that passwords are never to be written down? You can't just write down a user name and password and stick it on your monitor. That is a serious violation. What's wrong with you? Are you totally incompetent?"

"Are you here to insult me?"

"I'm here to do my job and protect people's private information."

"You're a bureaucrat. The job has gone to your head. What gives you the right to harass me like this?"

"Do you have a problem with the federal government?"

"Yes—it's satanic."

"Satanic?"

"You may not even know that you're being used. Or maybe you do."

"Please explain."

"I am a soldier in God's army. I stand for righteousness. You've been sent here as a demon to torment me."

"I can assure you that I'm not a demon sent from Satan to torment you."

Charles arrived at work late and gave the two a look of incredulity as he passed them and sat at his desk.

"How often do you perceive people as being demonic?" Conomikes asked.

"There are two types of people in the world, those who serve God and those who are Satan's hands on earth."

"Are some people able to listen to your thoughts?"

Ulysses made a tremulous exhalation and darted his eyes around. "Yes, but I'm not going to let you into my head."

"Do you think I'm one of those people you talk about, Satan's hands on earth?"

"I think so."

"And do you think I can read your thoughts?"

"Possibly—but I'm jamming your transmissions right now."

"How are you doing that?"

"I'm not telling you."

"I see. Do you know what ISP masking is?"

"Yes, but I don't do it."

"Do you monitor your coworkers, trying to determine which ones are part of God's army and which are Satan's hands on earth?"

"No."

"Do you have reason to believe there is anyone in your organization listening to your thoughts?"

Ulysses shook his head in frustration. "All these HIPAA policy questions are simply a ploy for you to harass me. I think you need to realize that you can't defeat me. You should be leaving now."

"Is that a personal external hard drive plugged into your computer?"

"Yes, it is."

"Can we look at the contents of that drive?"

Ulysses unplugged the cable from the computer and wrapped it around the hard drive and then put it into his briefcase. He picked it up and stood, collecting his keys from off the desk.

"I'm leaving early."

"Okay, fine," said Charles.

After he had walked out of the room, Conomikes turned to Charles.

"Is he always like that?"

"Since I first met him, he's been a paranoid shithead, but I've never heard that Satan stuff before."

"You apply a little stress and the true colors always come out."

Conomikes went to the executive wing of the building and entered the office of the chief operating officer.

"Was our network guy able to help you with your questions?" asked the COO.

"I have a serious matter I need to discuss with you," Conomikes said. "Can I close the door?"

"Yes, what seems to be the matter?"

Conomikes shut the door and walked over to a wall of frames.

"Is this all your rock band memorabilia?"

"Yes, authentic signatures. I actually know a lot of those people. Can you tell me what's wrong?"

Conomikes turned to him. "You may want to get your CEO."

"He's away. Besides, I'm the one running the company. He's good at getting investors to pour capital into us. I do everything else."

"All right—from my questioning of Ulysses Garcia, it became apparent that he's been stealing electronic company property. When I asked to see what was on his external hard drive. He packed it away in his briefcase and left the building in a hurry."

"He what?"

"There is also a chance that he could be involved in an identity theft ring that could bring fines to your company in the excess of a million dollars annually. I should inform my agency that an investigation of your company is needed."

"A million dollars?"

"That's nothing—once the news gets out—the lawsuits from all the people who have had their personal information exposed to cyber villains will inundate you like fleas on a mutt. However, being a former business person myself, I'd hate to see the wrath of federal agencies descend upon you."

"What do you suggest?"

"Perhaps I don't really need to write up this report if you treat this as simple case of employee theft. If you call the Fort Lauderdale Police Department and accuse Mr. Garcia of taking home company material, they could get a warrant and search his external hard drive. Then it really wouldn't have to be a matter of our agency fining you. You were proactive and stopped the bad guy. That looks pretty good."

"Call the cops and you won't write us up?"

"Here's the number of someone that will be sure to protect your interests. He'll make sure things work out in your favor."

The COO took the business card. "This is a homicide detective."

"Don't worry about that. He's pro-business, if you know what I mean. As government workers, we can be real assholes. But I'm a bit more lenient. The next time I come, I'm going to throw the book at you if you don't get your HIPAA policies in order, understood?"

"Yes."

"Good."

"I make a phone call and this nightmare goes away?"

"Too good to be true?"

"Thanks for doing this. I promise we'll get all our policies straight."

When Conomikes stepped outside the building he made a call.

"Hey Ryan, you were right. They bought my old expired agency ID …Listen, this Ulysses guy is a complete lunatic—thinks people can hear his thoughts—the whole nine yards. Expect a call from a nervous business executive in a few minutes."

"Thanks for sticking your neck out for me," Salter said.

"I hope you get this crazy murdering piece of shit."

# CHAPTER NINETEEN

"He's in the box," Hector raised his eyebrows.

"Good," Salter said as he walked down the hallway with a large catalog envelope and a tablet device under his arm. He stepped into the interrogation room to find Ulysses staring at the blank wall.

"Mr. Garcia," Salter said. "I'm Ryan Salter. Can I get you anything to eat?"

"What do you have?" Ulysses asked.

"I can get you a candy bar out of the vending machine. Or what about chicken soup?—they sell that too."

"Chicken soup—that sounds good. I'll take that."

"Excellent, I'll be right back."

Salter walked out to the room and closed the door. "Can someone get me some chicken soup? I'm going to kill him with kindness."

Ostroff, Noriega and Ramos stood by Salter watching Ulysses on a television screen.

"God, I hope he doesn't lawyer up," Noriega said.

"He might," Ramos said. "You should have heard him talking about his constitutional rights when we first wanted to talk to him."

"Let's keep our fingers crossed," Salter said. "But he strikes me as the typical guilty person that'll waive all their rights because they're so curious to find out what the police know."

"We don't know much," Ramos said. "How're you going to do this?"

"Watch me carefully," Salter said. "I'm going to ask normal questions to get an emotional baseline. I'll also show interest in anything he wants to talk about in order to get him to open up. Then if he starts with any unusual body language, we know he's lying. The nerves will give him away and he'll get thirsty—eyes will get dry and he'll blink more. He'll turn white like he's scared. If he needs to convince me—to explain something in a lot of detail, instead of simply giving me simple yes and no answers—he's probably lying. I'll just keep asking questions and slowly turn up the heat and hit him with dead silence if I have to. If he gives me even a shred of candor, I'll minimize the crime and appear sympathetic. We need a confession. We don't have any physical evidence. But—suppose we do get a confession. If this guy is really nuts, that sets the stage for an insanity defense. I'll do what I can to establish that he understands the difference between right and wrong."

Noriega squinted at the monitor. "What's he doing?"

"Talking to himself," Ostroff said. "What does it look like he's doing? He probably hears voices too."

"God help us."

A uniformed officer arrived with a steaming container of soup. "I microwaved it."

"Thanks," Salter said and went back into the room.

"Here you are," he said.

"Thank you," Ulysses replied.

Salter pulled his chair close and tried to convey sincerity with hand gestures. "I'm sorry we have to do all this. I have some things I need to tell you and some things I should share with you—and I want to hear your side of the story, but the only way I can do this is to first read you your Miranda rights. Are you with me so far?"

"Yes."

"Okay, I'm just going to read it from this card. We have a lot to talk about, but I can't say anything unless you waive this warning. I really need you to waive your rights so we can talk. All right, I'm going to read the warning now. Here goes—You have the right to remain silent. Anything you say can and will be used against you in court. You have the right to consult with an attorney before making any statement and to have an attorney present during questioning. If you want an attorney, but can't afford one, an attorney will be appointed for you free of charge. You may stop the questioning at any time—do you waive your rights at this time?"

"Yes."

"Okay, I just need your signature right here," Salter took a form out of the envelope and placed it on top for him to sign.

"Is there anything else I can get you? How's the soup?"

"Salty," Ulysses said after the first spoonful.

"They put so much damn sodium in those things. You ever wonder why they do that? It's not healthy. Everyone knows that."

"That's exactly right," Ulysses said. "There are thousands of government documents proving that the population is intentionally being sickened and sterilized as part of a mass eugenics program. Not only are our foods unhealthy, they're adding toxins and hormones. They're creating genetically modified foods that are linked to organ failure."

"I think I heard something about that," Salter feigned interest.

"They're going to kill eighty to ninety percent of the earth's population. In another generation practically the entire human race is going to be sterile. It's a population reduction program."

"Why are they doing this?"

"The powers that be want the earth to themselves. Why do you think they're dumping toxic petroleum waste on the crop fields? Why do you think the airplanes are spraying the cities with chemical agents?

"They're trying to kill us."

"Exactly. So tell everyone you know not to let their kids eat all these foods with chemicals. Warn them."

"I will. But do you really think it's a worldwide conspiracy? It could just be companies trying to find ways to make more money by doing everything in a more cost effective manner."

"That's what my wife thinks. But it is a conspiracy. If you only knew what was really going on."

"What's going on?"

"Are you a religious person?"

"Somewhat."

"There are dark forces present in the world today. It's ironic that we call them dark, because actually they're beings of light. The name Lucifer literally means light-bringing. He is the one that controls the global elite and secret societies. They are behind the population reduction program."

"They think they're better than everyone else and want to get rid of the masses."

"Yes, they're devising ways to make us sick and ultimately kill us."

"What can be done about this?"

"The first thing is to educate ourselves and learn to see the signs."

"What signs?"

"Occult and illuminati type symbols—and predictive programming?"

"What is that?"

"They prepare the population for upcoming events through subliminal means, usually through the media."

"Can you give me an example?"

"Look at all the dystopian movies that come out. It's to prepare us for the collapse of civilization."

"Do you think it will happen?"

"It's inevitable."

"But you're still trying to do what you can to prevent this, right?"

Ulysses looked down for a moment. "Yes."

"Is it then just a matter of principle fighting against what is inevitable?"

"In a sense, that is true. What's important is to be fighting on the correct side."

"Which side is that?"

"The side of righteousness—at the moment this world comes to an end, I want to be found with my hands around the neck of the enemy."

"Strangling them to death-"

"Yes."

"Would you consider doing something like this before the end of the world?"

"I'm speaking figuratively."

"So you wouldn't literally strangle anyone?"

"I don't think so."

"Interesting—well, let us start. Do you know why you're here today?"

"I suspect it had something to do with the federal agent that came to see me yesterday at work. He's a typical government bureaucrat, throwing his weight around and oppressing the people. He was probably incensed that someone would dare stand up to him like I did, so he called the police on me. Who knows what kind of fake information was planted on my devices."

"You're a network administrator, correct?"

"That's right."

"But you're also a software engineer. Wouldn't you make more money programming than maintaining the network?"

"Yes, but I don't like all the meetings. There's too much to discuss when working on projects."

"You don't really like working with others."

"Not really."

"Would you call yourself a loner?"

"I suppose you could call me that."

"Do sometimes people get the wrong idea about you? Perhaps, they assume that your quiet nature is somehow a form of hostility."

"It's possible."

"Could the federal agent have gotten the wrong impression about you? Did he take offense and decide to treat you unfairly?"

"It could be that, or it might be something much more sinister."

"Sinister—like what?"

"He may be the hands of Satan."

"Why do you think that?"

"It has to do with what I've been telling you. The forces of darkness and their occult secret societies are waging war against us."

"Well I'm glad I can hear your side of the story. Maybe it's the federal agent that needs to be investigated. Perhaps he's abusing his power. Maybe I can help you. What do you think about that?"

"I've done nothing wrong."

"And maybe he planted things on the drive that you took home. Would you like to know what police found on it?"

"What?"

Salter awoke the tablet from sleep mode and turned it around for Ulysses to see. A folder with large thumbnail icons displayed Emily Patrick's photos taken in Japan.

"These pictures belonged to one of your coworkers. She took quite a few selfies. That's because she went to Japan by herself. I'm sure you were shocked to hear about her death."

"I was."

"Could you tell me why you were in possession of these images?"

Ulysses scratched his neck. "I was saving them."

"Saving them for what?"

"I was thinking about making a tribute for her."

"Like a slideshow or something like that?"

"Yeah, something like that."

"And how did you get these images?"

Ulysses let out a long breath. "Are you suspecting me of her murder?"

"I'm just wondering how these images got on your device."

"I didn't kill Emily Patrick."

"Okay—just for my curiosity, how did the images get-"

"If you don't believe me, I'll take a polygraph."

"You'll take a polygraph? You would do that?"

"Yes, I would."

A short time later, Salter was in the hallway with the polygraph examiner, looking through a window in the door at a seated Ulysses.

"He doesn't want to do it," said the examiner.

"What?"

"I put the tubes around him, the blood pressure cuff and the sensors on his fingers. You told me that he was paranoid, so I assured him that nothing was going to shock or hurt him. I didn't even get a chance to ask him his name. All of sudden, he tells me that he doesn't want to do it anymore."

"Shit."

"You think he's a killer?"

"He's all I've got. I wonder if he was stalling. I asked him how the pictures of the victim came into his possession. Maybe this lie detector field trip was to give him time to think of an answer."

"Pictures don't prove anything."

Salter sighed. "It's possible that he's just a paranoid person with a crush on a coworker. But he did have the opportunity to install surveillance software on her phone, stalk her and murder her."

"So he probably did it."

"It has to be him."

After Ulysses was brought back to the interrogation room, Salter went to his office and threw a chair against the wall.

Ramos looked at him in shock. "What's wrong?"

"I'm pissed! First he says he'll take a polygraph and then he changes his mind."

"Are you okay?"

"He can't see that I'm upset." Salter took deep breaths through his nose and let them out moving his hands harmoniously. He walked back in the interrogation room and gave Ulysses a polite smile.

"I'm sorry about that," Ulysses said.

"What happened?" Salter said. "I thought you were going to take the polygraph test."

"The more I thought about it, the more I realized that they could figure out some way to harm me."

"The tests are perfectly safe."

"You never know."

"Okay—back to the pictures. How did they get on your device?"

"Please understand that what I'm about to tell you has enormous implications regarding everything we know about the world we live in and every aspect of our lives."

"All right, go on."

"I felt personally responsible for what happened to Emily."

"You do?"

"I should have seen this coming. She was involved in a dark world of secret societies and organized crime. I had been worried about her for quite some time. The reason I didn't want to say anything before was because of the laws regarding the violation of personal privacy. I had been monitoring her to see what I could find out about the dangerous world that she had entangled herself in."

"You should have notified the police."

"There's no one I can trust."

Salter rubbed his head and tried to hide his frustration. "What can you tell me about this dark world that she was involved with?"

"There is a man named Toshi Yamamoto. He is a member of the Japanese aristocracy. He has ties to the Li family of China. The Li family controls a secret society of organized crime known as the Triads. I suspect that Emily got caught up in this hierarchy of evil and paid the ultimate price."

"The Triads-"

"They're all over the world. Isn't it funny that after spending time with Toshi Yamamoto, Emily was killed? Mr. Yamamoto is the person you should be questioning. Ask him if he's ever been to China. You'll find that behind the layers of secrecy and deception are all the truths you're searching for."

"You want me to ask him if he's ever been to China?"

"Yes, that simple question will cause everything to unravel. You'll solve your mystery."

"Okay, this is just a formality. Let me just get this out of the way. I'm going to ask you a few questions, just so we have it for the record. Did you kill Emily Patrick?"

"No."

"Did you harm her in any way?"

"No."

"Were you attracted to Emily?"

"She was an attractive woman."

"But were you attracted to her?"

"I may have been a little attracted to her."

"How much is a little?"

"I wasn't in love with her."

"Were you infatuated with her?"

"No."

"Did you like staring at pictures of her? Did you obsess over her? Did you want to get your hands on her?

"No."

"Did you want to get your hands around her? Did you want to get your hands around her neck?"

"No! I didn't kill her! Toshi Yamamoto killed her!"

"Why are you so certain it was him?"

"Because he's a prince—a dark prince."

"Admit it. It was you. You killed her!"

"No!"

"Yes it was! Admit it!"

"I want a lawyer!"

Salter heaved a sigh. "There's no need for a lawyer. You're free to go."

# CHAPTER TWENTY

Ulysses and his stepson, Robby, were watching television while Melanie was out shopping for groceries. Ulysses grew agitated as the cartoon character pronounced the Mandarin greeting, ni hao. A host of jungle animals joined in singing the words and dancing. He paused the DVR.

"Why did you stop it?" Robby asked.

"We need to talk," Ulysses said. "There is a reason that they want you to learn Chinese. The east is the land of Buddha and Krishna—false gods. You have to protect yourself from all the dangers out there. The world is evil. Everything in existence is trying to kill you. You don't believe me? Let me give you an example. Suppose you were on a plane and it crashed into a jungle. People think that nature is good, but the opposite is true. Within minutes, all kinds of insects would start to lay eggs in your cuts and scratches. Perhaps you only sustained minor injuries when the plane went down, but these minor scrapes would soon become infected and all kinds of organisms would start to grow in them. The mosquitos carry malaria—so there's a good chance that you would die from that. Or you could get very sick from drinking the water. Oh, the water may look clean, but it is full of bacteria. Of course, there would be predators looking to tear you to pieces, and yes large anacondas or jaguars could do this, but it's the little ones that you have to particularly be on the lookout for. Tiny venomous frogs and snakes are your worst enemies. But there is also the weather to consider. You could drown in heavy rains and flash flooding. Well, if the crocs don't get you first. Did I mention that there are poisonous plants that can paralyze you, stop your breathing, but keep your heart beating so you can be conscious and suffer until the very last moment? And everything I just described is of the natural world. Nature is not good. It is your enemy. But humans are even worse than jungles or rainforests. The indigenous people might shoot arrows or throw spears at you. They might even chop off your head and turn it into an object that can be used in a ritual of some sort. Or they may just want it as a trophy. However, let me give you another scenario. Your plane doesn't crash in a jungle. Suppose one of the pilots intentionally steers the plane right into a mountain. This actually happened once. Personally, I believe that aliens transmitted the orders to kill into his brain. The plane was probably being followed by UFO's. Or maybe it had nothing to do with aliens. Perhaps the man simply wanted to kill lots of people. Humans are evil. Don't forget this. But there is something even more frightening and terrible than any of the things I just mentioned. Do you know what that is?"

"No," said Robby.

"Eternal damnation—if you are on the side of the devil, you will be thrown into a lake of fire for all eternity. Forever and ever you will burn and scream in agony. Can you imagine that—screaming in the worst pain possible for billions of years? The serpent is very crafty. He will trick you into serving him. If you're not careful—if you don't try as hard as you possibly can to resist the schemes of the enemy—you will burn and scream forever and ever. Don't ever forget what I've just told you. The world and everything in it are evil. There is danger everywhere. Try as hard as you can not to be fooled by Satan. You must be smart. If you're not, you could go to hell. You could be a holy man and do everything perfect until the very last minute of your life. But with one minute left to live, you could develop dementia and lose your mind. The enemy could come and trick you into aligning yourself with the world. You might think to yourself, this isn't so bad. The singers and dancers are talented, the books are interesting, and the trees are pretty—it is a beautiful world. And just then, you have fallen in love with this evil world. God will punish you severely for this. People try to paint a picture of a loving god, but our God commanded the total destruction of the Canaanites. Every man, woman, child, animal, plant and living thing was to be killed. The kings of all the cities were to have their necks stepped on and put to the sword. Why? Because they were evil. They were very evil. But it's not so different today. The people are still evil. I hope you always remember the things I have just told you. There is danger everywhere. The world is evil. I don't care what anyone else says. I know what I'm talking about. Someone like Pastor Bill might say that I'm twisting and perverting the word of God. What people like him need to understand is that the scripture has to be taken literally. All this fuzzy logic and postmodern relativism you hear people talking about are lies from the pit of hell. There is light and dark, good and bad. There is nothing in between. If you are deceived—if you align yourself with the aliens and the illuminati and all the demons—you're going to hell."

"The frogs and snakes have poison?" Robby asked.

"I think the blue frogs are the most poisonous," Ulysses nodded. "Just a tiny amount of poison can kill twenty humans. Jellyfish are also venomous, so are scorpions and spiders. Even snails can kill you with their neurotoxins. I want you to be very careful. I'm going to speak to you like a grownup. First of all, you need to understand that what happened yesterday proves that we are in danger. I'm a very important person, Robby. I know a lot of things. And because I know a lot of things, I'm being persecuted. Ultimately, they want to destroy me—destroy us. I want you to be alert and prepared to do whatever is necessary to protect yourself. Suppose someone offers you sugar to put on your food. Did you know that potassium cyanide looks just like sugar? Once you ingest it, your stomach acid will convert it into hydrogen cyanide. Your body's cells won't be able to use oxygen anymore. You'll slowly die of asphyxiation—an excruciatingly painful death. But there are much worse things than potassium cyanide. Someone might poison you with polonium-210 or dioxin. Or much worse, someone could torture you for weeks before killing you. People do terrible things sometimes. I believe it is mind control. There is a force that transmits information into our brains. In medieval times, they would make people sit on glowing hot metal chairs and wear glowing hot metal crowns. As the person died and his flesh cooked, others would come to eat him. Why would they do such things? Their minds had been taken over by malevolent forces. Not that long ago, there was a man named Dahmer who also ate people. He even once poured acid through a hole in a skull that he had drilled. The person woke up, and later he did things that you're not old enough to know. Anyway, the point I'm trying to make is that even if people seem good, at any moment evil could come into them and control their minds.

And what they're capable of doing to you is beyond comprehension. I'm still trying to determine what happened to Karmic type Li. She could hear my thoughts, so something had to be done. But who did what? Was it me, a soldier in God's army, manifesting divine righteous wrath? Or was it Yamamoto? That is what I would like to know."

"Is the sugar in my cereal okay?"

"It's not healthy, but you can eat it. Just don't accept sugar or anything from strangers."

"The cereal isn't good?"

"Robby—Robby—have you not heard anything I've been telling you? The world and everything in it is bad. I'm not going to argue with your mother about what cereal you eat, but I just want you to know that—no—it's not good for you. They're trying to sicken and kill the people in order to reduce the population."

"The cereal is going to kill me?"

"Probably not, but if you keep eating the foods that they want you to eat you'll become sterile."

"What's that?"

"Sterility—you won't be able to make babies."

"How do you make babies?"

"Oh God—I don't know how much of what I'm saying you can understand. You don't even know where babies come from. I'm sure Yamamoto thinks this is funny. He's probably watching us right now and laughing."

Melanie came home carrying several bags of groceries. She glanced at Ulysses and Robby and went into the kitchen. After the louder than usual slamming of cabinets, Ulysses went to gauge her mood.

"Hey," he said.

Melanie ignored him as she hurried to get the frozen foods in the freezer.

"The silent treatment?"

She glared at him, let out an angry sigh and resumed cramming cold bags of vegetables together next to the ice maker.

"You're acting like a child," he said.

"I'm acting like a child?" she responded.

"There's no reason to be acting this way-"

"You were arrested and lost your job yesterday. You want to act like everything is okay? Things are not okay."

Ulysses rolled his eyes. "I've been through hell and back, but instead of having a wife that stands by me, I have to put up with this."

"How can I stand by you when everything that comes out of your mouth is pure bullshit?"

"Bullshit? How can you say that?"

"Nothing you told me about what happened yesterday makes sense."

"Yes it does make sense! An agent from the U.S. Dept. of Health and Human Resources came to ask me about the company's HIPAA policies. He was a complete asshole. He just wanted to badger and yell at me. When I stood up to him and told him that no one talks to me like that, he decided that he would ruin my life. Why?—Just because he has the power to ruin lives. So he did just that. Don't worry. I'll just get another job. I'm probably overqualified for most tech jobs, but oh well."

"Maybe this is a blessing in disguise. You're a software engineer. You should be making a lot of money, instead of pretending to be a Geek Squad guy fixing computers."

"I didn't just fix computers—I managed the entire corporate network. I made sure that that everything was being hosted by the proper servers. Just the other day, I planned the most perfect way to expand our external hosting sources. You know we pay a $25,000 license just to have all our code libraries hosted somewhere? We have all kinds of licenses like that. If something were to happen to one server, there would be significant redundancy in place—because of me—me."

"I don't understand anything you just said, but they didn't pay you hardly anything. And you're talking like you still work there. All this stuff is meaningless. What's wrong with you? Are you clueless? Who cares what licenses there are? Have you even started working on your resume yet?"

"No."

"Why not?"

"I'm recovering from yesterday. I just need a day for my nerves to settle."

"Work on your resume. Don't tell them too much about the networking stuff. You're a world class software engineer. We should be rich and living in a big house. But I don't really think you care about your family."

"There are more important things going on in the world."

"Don't you—even for one second—don't you dare start talking to me about your conspiracy theories."

"Fine—I'll work on my resume and land a high paying job so you can have your big house and all the material things you covet."

"Don't try to twist this around and make it sound like I'm a greedy bitch. I've put up with your lack of ambition for years and never said anything."

"Yeah, I'm surprised it took you this long to tell me how much you love money."

Robby walked into the kitchen. "The food is very bad for you," he said. He slowly left the room with his head down.

"My God—look what you've done," Melanie said.

"It's for his own good. The sooner he realizes that the world is evil, the better."

"Don't think I bought any organic food. With you out of work, I'm not going spend the money. We'll just have to wash everything well to get the pesticides off."

"It's much more than pesticides. We're talking about eugenics. There are deadly toxins in the food—mercury and all kinds of things linked with brain tumors and organ failure. Instead of spending less money, we should be investing in emergency food supplies."

"Emergency food supplies?"

"I was looking into it. A six month supply from the Patriotic Glory Survivalist website would give us non GMO food with a twenty five year shelf life for less than a thousand dollars. A year supply would be less than eighteen hundred. A lot of it sounds delicious—lasagna, corn chowder, chocolate pudding-"

"What on God's green earth are we going to do with food that lasts for twenty five years?"

"They come in large stackable containers."

"This has to do with all your end of the world stupidity-"

"No, it's not stupid—they've got energy drink mix, whey powder, mashed potatoes. We might even get free t-shirts."

"Yules—we live in South Florida! There are no basements. We can't crawl into some underground bunker filled with survivalist supplies in case someone decides to nuke us. This makes absolutely no sense!"

"We might survive an atomic blast. We live way out in the

suburbs. Or it could be a dirty bomb. The Patriotic Glory Survivalist website also has nuclear and biological products—potassium iodine tablets to absorb radioactivity in case a nuke does go off or the Turkey Point nuclear reactor has a meltdown. They've got particle masks and radiation emergency kits-"

"Yules-"

"I've put a lot of thought into this. There are so many things that could happen—Ebola, famine, natural disasters, nuclear war, the collapse of civilization-"

"Yules-"

"We should get walkie-talkies and gas masks. And you should go to the gun range with me. We need to practice, practice, practice."

"Why can't you just be normal? Why do you have to be so afraid?"

"Do you really want to take the risk of being unprepared? The problem with people is that they become complacent. Just because something catastrophic hasn't happened in a while doesn't mean it couldn't happen tomorrow."

"Just listen to yourself. You're unemployed and need to make job hunting your top priority. Instead, you're talking like someone that's been watching too many post-apocalyptic movies."

Robby came back into the kitchen. "Ulysses knows a lot of things and that's why the bad people are after him," he said.

Melanie shook her head. "I'm not leaving my son alone with you anymore."

# CHAPTER TWENTY ONE

Margo seemed to arrive within minutes of his text.

"What's wrong?" she said. "You seem like something is bothering you."

"I can't really discuss an ongoing case," Salter said.

"You don't care much for rules."

"You have a point."

"So talk to me."

"I'm dealing with a mentally ill suspect with a high IQ. He got the better of me yesterday. First, he says that he's willing to take a polygraph. He's strapped in and ready to go, but then at the last minute he changes his mind. I take him back to the interrogation room and after a short while I got frustrated—started yelling at the guy to admit they he committed a murder. Of course, he lawyers up. Usually, I'm very patient. I make people think that I'm the best friend they ever had. I give them the kind of attention and interest they've been craving since they were toddlers. It's almost inevitable that they start telling me their entire life story. But this guy is getting away with murder. I don't know what to do. I can't make this case my top priority forever. There are lots of crimes to solve. If you don't make any progress in the first few days, you have to move on to something else."

"All right so tell me everything about this guy."

"Hmm—he's paranoid and thinks all kinds of crazy shit. I don't know what he's so afraid of. Everyone should be afraid of *him*. He obsesses over a girl, cyberstalks her and strangles her, leaving no evidence. We did find that the surveillance software had been removed from her phone. But there is nothing that proves that he did it. He had photos of the victim in his possession, but that doesn't prove murder. When I questioned him, he told me that he believed the victim was involved somehow in secret societies and organized crime. He seemed to know a lot about Toshi Yamamoto, the young man that the victim had met the night she was killed. He believed that Mr. Yamamoto was involved with an organized crime syndicate in China, despite being Japanese, not Chinese. He wanted me to ask Mr. Yamamoto if he had ever been to China. It's almost as if he believes that Yamamoto was the murderer. Obviously, it's just an attempt to cast suspicion on someone else. But I'd love to know what is going on. Why is the suspect obsessing about secret societies and such?"

"Are there really secret societies?" she asked.

"I guess any group that meets to talk about personal things is a secret society."

"Like us?"

"More like rich people who can't trust anyone."

She raised her eyebrows. "I hear it's not easy being rich. Everyone wants to sue or extort money from you."

"Why are people like that?"

"You're asking me? You're the detective."

"What do you know about China and Japan?" he asked.

"One is big like the US. The other is the size of California."

"My partner's been to all those places."

"The one you have the hots for?

"Yeah, that one. I'm going to give her a call. Do you mind?"

"I suppose it's okay," she smiled.

Salter selected Ramos' photo from his contacts and pressed the dial icon on his phone.

"Hey," Ramos said.

"What's in China?" Salter said.

"What do you mean?" she said.

"Emily Patrick was obsessed with Japan. Ulysses was obsessed with Emily Patrick. Now he's obsessed with a Japanese man named Toshi Yamamoto. He's also obsessed with China. What's the connection?"

"Let's see—Japan gets a lot of its culture and traditions from China. The two countries have also had a lot of bad history. But many Chinese and Japanese are friendly towards each other. A lot of

Japanese had been living and working in China because of the great recession. That wouldn't have much to do with Mr. Yamamoto since he's rich—unless he really has something to do with the Chinese Triads. But, we are dealing with Ulysses Garcia, someone who's not right in his head. I think he's just giving us garbage, if you ask me."

"There's really nothing there, is there?

"I could spend a few hours threading through Google trying to find something."

"Could you?"

"Okay."

"Bye."

"Bye."

Margo narrowed her eyes. "Was it nice talking to her?"

"Shut up," Salter laughed.

"I don't understand—the suspect had lots of pictures of the girl he killed. Isn't that enough to prove he was the weirdo stalking her?"

"I'll give you an example. Suppose you were obsessed with me. Suppose you had saved pictures of me on your computer to look at. Suppose someone killed me. Do you think that it's fair that you should be accused of murder because you had some crush on someone?"

"No."

"That's why you can't convict someone based on appearances."

"I like the analogy you use. Do you think I'm obsessed with you?"

"You'd love to figure me out," he said.

"I'm very intrigued by you," she said. "Answer me this. Why is it that you want so badly to be alone?"

"I told you. I don't want anyone to get hurt."

"What happened? Why are you so careful not to hurt anyone's feelings?"

"It's just better that way. I like to be alone. I don't have any guy friends. Men usually talk about sports and politics. All I really care about are homicides. And women—I love women. So I don't want to do anything that would cause them pain. But I love to be around them. You've ever heard the expression that men and women can't just be friends?"

"Yeah."

"I wonder if it's true. I had a close female friend once. One day, she stopped returning my calls and emails. Over the course of a week, I tried to contact her many times. Finally, she sent me a message. She said that she couldn't go on pretending anymore—she no longer had romantic feelings for me. It just sort of came out of the blue and I wasn't really prepared for that. I don't know why, but that affected me. I experienced low mood for a while-"

"You mean you were depressed."

"Low mood."

"Guys can't admit when they're depressed."

"Depression, low mood, whatever—It just made me realize how incredibly rare it is to find a friend. People usually want something."

"You weren't attracted to your female friend?"

"Sometimes you just want a friend."

"I'm going now."

"Leaving?"

"Forever."

"Forever?"

"I just can't pretend anymore. I no longer have romantic feelings for you."

# CHAPTER TWENTY TWO

"Are you all right?" Kim Ramos asked.

Salter turned away from his desk to look at her. "I'm okay."

"You seem kind of down."

"I do?"

"Yeah, you do."

"You know how sometimes you shrug something off and refuse to let it affect you, but it's still there somewhere in your subconscious, poking around and being a nuisance?

"I think so."

"It's like that."

"You don't really want me to ask, right?"

"No," he smiled sadly.

Ramos turned back to her computer monitor and read an article about the complicated and potentially combustible relationship between the US, Japan and China.

"This stuff just goes on and on in a million different directions."

"I think we're just wasting time," Salter said. "Sorry—I'm a little obsessive in that regard. If we had an unlimited amount of time, I would research everything—even find someone in the US Foreign service to pick their brain for a day. I keep forgetting that we're dealing with a mentally ill person who's giving us shit right out of his fantasy world."

"So what do we do?"

"Go through the motions, I suppose. Mr. Garcia said that we should ask Mr. Yamamoto if he had ever been to China. He said that that simple question would cause a mystery to unravel. Let's pay him a visit. We'll ask him the question. Maybe it'll yield something. Stranger things have happened."

"Sounds good—Are you sure you're okay?"

"Eh—wimmin problems."

"I'm a woman. Maybe I can help you understand them."

"Men and women aren't that hard to understand. *I'm* the problem."

"I see."

Salter and Ramos were traversing Broward County and entering Dade via I-95. Despite waiting until the morning rush had ended, there were long delays. Accidents and construction competed against each other to create traffic congestion. The so-called car pool lanes were closed for some reason, contributing to the bottleneck of movement.

"I hate coming to Miami," Salter said.

"I don't like big cities either," Ramos said.

"Did you call Mr. Yamamoto and tell him we're coming."

"Yeah, but I hate to make him wait all day while we sit in traffic."

"Do you think there's any chance that Ulysses is right—even a .01 chance?"

"No," Ramos laughed.

"Me neither. Mr. Garcia is paranoid and delusional."

"People like that—even if they're only a little bit paranoid—are going to have a hard time functioning in the world we live in today."

Salter brooded. "What do you mean?"

"There's no personal privacy anymore. Everyone's on social networks. Our personal information is sold for profit. There are surveillance cameras everywhere. Not just on traffic lights—mannequins, vending machines and billboards. Supermarkets have facial recognition—it's even connected to social media. Our phone apps—God knows what's on them. Everything we do. Every website we go on—everything is being tracked. Imagine if you're a paranoid schizophrenic. It used to be that if you thought you were constantly being watched, you were labeled delusional. But now it's the truth. We are being watched. People who are truly sick are going to be pushed over the edge."

"So there'll be more people lashing out against perceived threats," he said.

"Exactly. And can you imagine someone like that listening to the conspiracy theory nuts on the internet?"

"The world becomes a dark place of secret societies and demonic plots."

"I wonder if that happened to our friend Ulysses Garcia," Ramos raised her eyebrows. "Emily's encounter with a secret society and her friendship with Mr. Yamamoto scared the bejesus out of him."

"Classic case of fear aggression."

"Everyone is paranoid to some extent," she said.

"How's that?"

"The conservatives are afraid of government. The liberals are afraid of corporations. Of course, both have good reason to be paranoid, but the more extreme someone is—it only reveals how emotionally unbalanced they are."

"I appreciate what you bring to this team—your intelligence—psychology background. How do you like our unit so far?"

"Of the five homicide units, I think I'm fortunate to be on this one."

"You're not just saying that."

"No."

"I've never had such a strange case until you showed up. Are they all going to be like this from now on?"

"I hope not," Ramos smiled.

"Maybe we can solve this case so your first time won't be a bummer."

"Can we ask the FBI for help?"

"We can, but they'll do everything we already did, and it'll go real slow. They have to stop and ask for approval from Washington for most things. The Assistant U.S. Attorney tells them what they can do and who they can arrest."

"You ever consider becoming a special agent?"

"I'm too old now. The cutoff is thirty seven."

"What about all the traffic light cameras? Wouldn't they tell us exactly where Mr. Garcia was the night of Emily Patrick's death—second by second?"

"We can't have anything to do with street surveillance. The ACLU sued the departments of Justice and Homeland Security over that. There's a lot tied up in litigation right now—nothing we can do."

Ramos stared at the road for a while. "So what's happening with your women troubles?" she sighed.

Salter nodded quietly for a moment, biting his lip. "I feel almost as if someone had broken up with me. But nothing of the sort happened. It's hard to explain."

"You lose a part of yourself whenever a connection with another person is lost."

"When someone becomes like a friend to you, it sucks losing that friendship or whatever it was."

"Someone that was like a friend but not a friend?"

"I can't talk about it."

"I hope it wasn't too bad."

"I just really liked her."

"Sorry."

"Ah, it's nothing. At least I'm not like Mr. Yamamoto, finding someone amazing, slow dancing with her under the stars and then immediately losing her to a monster."

…

Toshi Yamamoto was once again at the convenience store with the clerk that reminded him a little of Emily. There was no one buying lottery tickets that day or any line at all. He made eye contact with the cashier for what seemed like a moment too long and then purchased a soda and bag of chips, paying with his black Dubai First Royal Master Card, trimmed in gold, featuring a .235-carat diamond in the center. When he stepped outside the store, the bottle of soda dripped with condensation from the heat. As he walked to his car, a man followed him. Toshi turned to look at him.

"Hi, can I talk to you for a moment?" Ulysses asked.

"You may," Toshi answered.

With one glance, Toshi had made several observations about Ulysses. First, he looked rather odd to be wearing a denim button down over a t-shirt in the South Florida heat. Yes, it was December, but a scorcher of a day. Second, eyeglasses generally make people look more intelligent. However, this was the rare exception when glasses actually had made a person look imbecilic. Perhaps it was the worst possible combination of the frames and the shape of his face. Third, he looked sickeningly familiar, like an old mortal enemy that refused to remain safely confined to the past.

"Do you know who I am?" Ulysses asked.

"I believe that I do. Tell me, what is the name of the person that we might have much in common with?"

Ulysses looked at Toshi for a moment without responding. "Emily Patrick," he finally said.

Toshi's eyes widened. "I knew we would eventually meet."

"We have a lot to discuss, don't we? Why don't you invite me to your palace? I've always wanted to see what a multimillion dollar home looks like."

"What's your name?" Toshi asked.

"Ulysses," he said.

"And you would like to see my home," Toshi said with a knowing look.

"We'll go in your Lexus," Ulysses said.

"You're concealing a firearm."

"Yes, I am."

A short time later, the two were across the General Douglas MacArthur Causeway, past the security gate into the estate of Toshi Yamamoto. Inside the home, the high ceilings contained a wall of bookshelves next to stairs that led up to a loft. Ulysses looked up and noticed the samurai armor and katanas filling the loft like the window of a department store. Other than the swords and suits of armor, the rest of Toshi's home had the usual western looking décor, leather sofas, paintings and a giant screen television. The interior was so large that despite a pool table, grand piano and enormous telescope, the house didn't seem cluttered, but actually appeared to look empty.

"We sit and talk," Ulysses said in a commanding tone.

Toshi sat on one of the sofas, and Ulysses sat across from him on the other side of a glass coffee table. He removed his gun from his pants and rested it on his lap.

"You know why I'm here," Ulysses said.

"You're here to kill me," Toshi answered.

"Besides that."

"I really don't know."

Ulysses sighed. "This is an interrogation."

"You should be the one being interrogated," Toshi said.

"Why?"

"Because you killed Emily."

"No, actually it was you."

"What do you mean?"

"Mind control."

Toshi looked at him in disbelief. "Mind control?"

"Yes, but I want to understand exactly how and why this happened," Ulysses said. "I also have many other questions for you, but let's begin with Emily. First of all, it was unavoidable what happened to her. She was too much of a threat. She could hear my thoughts. She was your way of getting to me. You are the source, and she was one of your far reaching tentacles. What you didn't anticipate was that I would find you and kill you."

"You're not well," Toshi said.

Ulysses appeared not to have heard him. "But before I do, you will tell me everything. The evening of your Koyosha meeting—the night that Emily was present and the two of you discussed traveling and fighting alongside one another through different dimensions, samurai lineage and super powers-"

Toshi shook his head. "When you were spying on us, it seems you had bad reception."

"I know what I heard," Ulysses said. "The two of you are not from this world."

"I don't know what to tell you," Toshi shrugged.

"You can start by telling me the real meaning of the ghost stories."

"Ghost stories?"

"Don't play dumb. Four stories were told. They were obviously told in a manner that would only be understood by so-called enlightened people. There are many levels in which things can be understood. Isn't that right? The mystics have their esoteric knowledge, which they shroud in symbolism. You will tell me the exact meaning of each story and explain what everything represents. If you, for one moment, tell me that something is not symbolic or that there is no deeper meaning to the story, I'll blow your head off. Do you understand?"

"Yes."

"The first story had to do with a man visiting his estranged wife. He catches her in the act of adultery. However, instead, he sees a room covered in blood. And then he sees a ghost. Explain in detail the meaning of this story."

"May I ask a question first?"

"Go ahead."

"You expect to hear about the illuminati, aliens, demons, the new world order and all those sorts of things."

"Yes, I do."

Toshi sighed. "All right."

He glared slightly at Ulysses, with enough restraint not to warrant a gunshot. He wondered if it would be an honorable execution with some form of dignity, or would there be torture? What would keep his foe from blowing out a knee cap if the words that left his mouth weren't adequate? He thought quickly, formulating a narrative to keep him alive for as long as possible. Perhaps, something would transpire to change his situation while resorting to lies and deception. He could establish a case for his pardon, carefully woven into the fabric of the altered ghost stories. Or perhaps he would simply tell the truth and create new knowledge for this world.

Above on the loft were the Japanese katanas in their scabbards. How he wanted to cut Ulysses in half with them. If it were a more cordial affair, he would tell Ulysses how incredibly sharp the edges of the swords were. He would explain in detail how the ancient craftsmen combined two different metals to make katanas razor sharp and incomprehensibly strong. He would explain how impossible it was to create these swords before the modern understanding of chemistry and the microscopic world, and yet they somehow achieved this amazing accomplishment anyway. He would explain that indeed, some swords were rated strong enough to cut more than one man in half. To avenge Emily's death, he would gladly slice Ulysses into a million pieces.

"All right," he said again. "I'll reveal to you all our secrets."

# CHAPTER TWENTY THREE

"A yūrei always wants something," Toshi said. "And that is why we tell spooky stories, because there is always something hidden, something more than what can be plainly seen. Namely, the spirit wishes to resolve an emotional conflict so it can break free from this world and unite with ancestors. When Federico Jafet told the story of the adulterous wife and the yūrei, he was remembering a painful time in his own life, the sudden loss of his first wife and child. Talking about something is a way for people to help themselves heal psychological scars. I could tell you more about Jafet's heartbreak and his wife's infidelity, but that's not what you're interested in hearing. You would like to hear the deeper meaning of the story as it relates to geopolitical socioeconomic conspiracies and the ultimate truth regarding malevolent forces and their war against humanity. Am I correct?"

"Yes—exactly," Ulysses said.

"The yūrei represents something that watches us from the cover of darkness. Its hatred of humanity has kept it captivated for eons plotting the destruction of the world. The brief flash of carnage that Jafet saw—the blood and guts covering the walls of the room—symbolized the war that is coming. Europe is preparing for mass civil unrest, economic collapse and race wars. There will be concentration camps as far as the eye can see. Millions will be exterminated. Right now, the global elite are secretly causing financial catastrophes in all the countries of the world. Russia, China and the US will have nuclear exchanges—the ICBM's will rain down all over the globe. People are already being euthanized. Children and the elderly are despised. Most will die and only those that are part of the new world order will remain. So, in short, the yūrei represents the globalists, which I am a member of. Is this the kind of thing that you wanted me to say?"

"Yes, but I know all these things. Tell me something I don't know."

Toshi took a deep breath and thought for a moment. "What you don't know or understand is mystical in nature. If I were to explain it to you, your non-mystical mind would be unable to grasp its meaning. However, since you've stated your intent to kill me and only wish to purge me of whatever knowledge might prove interesting, I'll reveal the secrets to you. Perhaps you may surprise me by understanding more than I thought you would. Otherwise, forgive me if I bore you."

"Tell me all your dark secrets," Ulysses said in an exasperated tone.

"As you know, the nature of evil is to triumph over good. You might think of children happily frolicking over grass hills with their pets, wearing smiles and eager to join the adults in a plentiful feast as something that is genuinely good. So what would it take to ruin this perfect picture? First, we would need to take all that is in equilibrium and alter it slightly. Normal human body temperature is 98.6 degrees Fahrenheit. Lower it to 95 degrees and a person will suffer from hypothermia. Raise it to 99.5 degrees and you call that a fever. In the same way, to do away with what is good only requires that we tip the scales slightly one way or another. Evil is simply anything out of balance. For instance, a person can suffer from debilitating low self-esteem, or become an arrogant tyrant with a god complex. Neither is good. This is what we're after, isn't it? So in order for evil to triumph over good in the world, extremes have to work their way into every facet of human life. Not just poverty and overconsumption, squalor and decadence, but a life so out of balance that the human race slowly becomes mad. Yet, these are only externals—material things we are considering. What we're really after is the minds and souls of earth's inhabitants. Are you with me so far?"

Ulysses nodded.

"The neurons in our brains process and transmit information through electrochemical signaling. Somehow through all this signaling, thoughts arise. The thoughts help us to function in this world, problem solve and avoid danger. In our heads there are bundles of thoughts—some that never really go away and become almost like a permanent structure. We call these thought bundles in our minds, and we even begin to associate ourselves with these thought bundles. The bundles becomes our identity. We adamantly believe that we are our minds, but we are not our minds."

"I don't like where this is going," Ulysses said. "You're trying to confuse me."

"It takes many an aspiring mystic a long time to accept this. It may even take ten years to admit that this is even a possibility, but what I'm trying to get at is that the mind can also be unbalanced, just like one's body temperature."

"But what does it matter if we are not our minds?"

"Because these thought bundles sometimes go out of control and cause great harm. For example, someone can be happy and at peace, but over time they are seduced by some radical cult or worldview and are much more susceptible to committing a crime. What was once a well-balanced mind—at peace—has become an unbalanced and dangerous one."

"You wouldn't be referring to me?" Ulysses asked.

"I would never dream of it," Toshi said.

"Finish making your point."

"It is really simple. In order for evil to reign over the world, humans need to subscribe to the mistaken notion that their identities and everything they are is nothing more than bundles of thoughts in their heads. This way, they'll endlessly obsess over the defense of their opinions and things that gratify their egos. Everyone will be miserable and argumentative. Instead of inner peace, humans will be addicted to drama. The wheels of the mind will never stop turning. People will be perpetually scheming, plotting, causing physical and emotional harm to others, all in the name of being right—thus validating their opinions. A mystic is someone who believes that we are more than brain activity. We may not have all the answers, but we intuitively sense that there is divine consciousness. We are consciousness and there is also divine consciousness, and somehow the two meet. The philosophers and theologians may have the better answers, but-"

"A mystic is not what you say," Ulysses said angrily. "Mystics are demonic. I'm not sure what point you're trying to make with brain activity and thinking—and I don't know if this is some clever attempt to trick me."

Toshi nodded to acknowledge the outburst.

"Enough of this—Tell me the meaning of the second story—the story that *you* told.

"The part about Ushio was real," Toshio said. "I really did have a friend in school that committed suicide. But-"

Toshi was silent for a moment.

"Go on," Ulysses said. His inflection was sharp as if goading an animal to proceed.

"What I said is true. I can see everyone I've ever had a close bond with who has stepped into the world of the dead. But on to the things you want to hear about—the globalists and their plans to destroy the world. Again, the yūrei represents the unknown, what we're afraid of. The hand coming out of the wall is symbolic of the powerful reach of we have—we—the elite, the secret societies."

The tension in Toshio's shoulders was beginning to manifest itself as a pain rising to his head. He wasn't sure how much longer he could continue his discourse of extemporaneous answers to questions from the realm of the absurd. The state of anxiety and heightened awareness was beginning to affect his nervous system, causing physical and mental exhaustion. *Tell him what he wants to hear. Buy time. The detectives are on their way. Opportunity may strike. There may be some way to escape this web*, he kept telling himself. But how long could he keep this up? What would he do when he ran out of ideas?

"There will be hundreds of millions dead," Toshi continued. "We have bioweapons labs all over the earth producing the agents of death we need to kill everybody. Yes, we are the demons you fear—releasing toxins into the atmosphere, in the water, deep into the soil. You're eating food that has been covered in infernal excrement. We're splicing thousands of species of animal embryos into human embryos. There will be no one left that is human. Mankind will disappear off this planet. It will be on earth as it is in hell."

"Exactly!" Ulysses said, unable to contain himself. "World War III will be here within the next few months. They're already training young teenagers to enforce martial law. The European nations are about to collapse. Our currency is going to be devalued. The US dollar will collapse and it'll be worth nothing. Everyone will be poor. No one will be able to afford to eat anymore. There will be mass famine. God will be removed from money, and they'll take our guns. While this is going on, a staged biological attack will kill half the US population. And that's not counting all the nuke attacks in major cities.

The flu attacks, bankruptcy and terror attacks will be staged by the government. It will happen on dates with the number eleven or some other number of satanic significance. And when it happens, the government will announce the existence of aliens, because they're the ones orchestrating everything. You're a part of all this. How can you live with yourself? Why? Why do you do this?"

Toshi combed through his hair with his fingers. He could sense an end coming. Ulysses had heard plenty. He seemed to be shifting his awareness towards judgment and condemnation. Toshi expected him to empty his gun at any moment. His only hope for more time was to remind him that there were more ghost stories and their proper exegesis was required.

"The reason I am a part of this can best be illustrated by the third story—the one that Father Osf told after I was finished with mine. Did you hear that one, or had you lost phone reception?"

"I heard it."

"Just curious, did you see any video or did you only turn on the phone's mike?"

"It was mostly audio."

Toshio smirked with displeasure. "Father Osf's story was kind of prophetic, don't you think?—an unstable man wanting to kill someone that represented something that he truly hated."

Ulysses pointed his gun at Toshi. "One more word like that and I'll end this. Tell me the meaning of the story as it relates to the globalists and the new world order."

"A man wants to enter the priesthood—not something his father fully supports. He finds that he cannot afford the tuition costs of seminary. He concludes that organized religion is evil and decides that he wants to kill a priest. On his way to the church he dies in a traffic accident. The ghost haunts Father Osf. He persuades him to give a sermon of sorts, repeating his words. What the ghost wants the world to know is why God does not consider the second day to be good—the day in which the sky was created. Why is the sky not good? Is the question that seems paramount, above all other things that a tormented soul is unable to let go of. The question ties him to this earthly plane. You may have heard it said that the reason God did not declare the second day to be good is because Lucifer is the prince of the power of the air, the spirit that is at work in the sons of disobedience, as scripture puts it. Some Christian radio evangelists interpret this to mean that the airwaves are evil, and therefore broadcasting television or radio is of the devil, which is funny because they themselves are also using the airwaves. However, perhaps there is some truth to this. The media, which you might think of as a proverbial whore of Babylon is driven by ratings and money. Reality is sensationalized and distorted until a negative view of the world is achieved. Sex sells, but negativity and fear mongering sell more. Just as food manufacturers add more and more sugar to their products to satisfy their addicted customers, the media gives people exactly what they want—a terrifying world. Fear is a form of arousal, and people crave this type of sensuality. There is good and bad in the world, but an unbalanced person sees only bad. And all it really takes is one crazy person to affect many others. Japan, where I was born, is one of the most secular countries in the world. There are shrines and temples everywhere, but on the whole, we're really not that religious. There are also quite a few Christian churches. Suppose you're intrigued by a particular religion, but you met a person that belonged to that belief system and found them to be a lunatic. Why would you want anything to do with that religion? And yet many are drawn to lunatics-"

"You're not telling me anything useful," Ulysses said. "Prepare to die."

"Wait—don't you want to hear the meaning of the last story—the one that Emily Patrick told? If I explain it to you—you'll understand everything."

"Fine—tell me."

"Hers was different because it was not about a ghost, but her dream body—an Ikiryō. She begins her story with an actual event—the day she was leaving Kyoto. A man helped her with the ticket vending machine at the subway. She instantly fell in love with this man, but as she was leaving she said she felt sick, as if she had just met the one person that she was destined to be with and would now lose him forever. As she traveled back to the States, her feelings worsened, eventually experiencing what we might call a break from reality. Whether she was actually losing her mind or simply falling into a deep depression—we do not know—but out of this came a most unusual occurrence, the separation of her soul from her body. Or you could say that she had found her astral body, or that it was simply an out of body experience—her consciousness free to roam around without any physical restraints. After a few nights of experimentation with her new abilities, she traveled back to Japan and found the man from the train station. She entered his mind and his fantasies and soon found that there is someone else she must compete with for access to his soul. The man had a deceased lover that is jealous and possessive. This ghost eventually tries to kill Emily, but she threatens to haunt the couple for all eternity. The next morning, Emily finds the knife that the ghost was going to kill her with by the side of the bed. In a sense, the knife is still there this very moment. In fact, the whole story represents something that is true and always keeps repeating itself."

"I'm tired of all this," Ulysses said. "I want to hear about the twenty families that are controlling the world and their plans to reduce the population. I want to hear about how the US military is preparing to slaughter millions of Americans. I want to hear about the plans for robots and drones to replace the dead humans and serve the globalists. I especially want to hear about your role with the Chinese triads and the establishment of the new world order."

"Would you like to hear about my trip to China?" Toshi asked.

"I would very much like to hear about that, as long as it's not a stall tactic."

Toshi looked at the ceiling to stretch his neck. "It was the year of the tiger."

"What year was that?"

"That was back in 2010. It seems like such a long time ago. It was the year of the World Expo, my first time in China. It was also the year that Shanghai officially had a Japanese expatriate group. There are many Japanese that follow what has been referred to the Shanghai dream, an opportunity to learn Mandarin, gain professional experience and return home with an enhanced resume. But as Japan became mired in recession, there wasn't much to come home to. A lot of Japanese were anxious, unsure of their future. Being a philanthropist, I went to China and tried to be supportive of the large Japanese community in Shanghai. I wanted to invest in Japanese businesses. There was even an art curator there that I wanted to talk to about funding the arts. It was the very first day that I was in Shanghai that I caught a glimpse of something perfect—something that proved to be the answer to everything."

# CHAPTER TWENTY FOUR

"I was looking down from my fifth story room at the Regal East Asia. It wasn't a five star hotel, but someone had recommended it. The people of the Tai chi class in the plaza were swaying like sea grass, as if welcoming me. Their hands caressed the air—offering passive resistance to the brute forces of life. And it was at this very moment when I yielded, when my heart was captured, overtaken, the way the hard is defeated by the soft. A short distance away from the Tai chi group, I saw a woman moving—slowly, gracefully. It took me a moment to realize that she wasn't performing Tai chi, but instead dancing a slow waltz with her arms embracing an invisible partner, gliding through her rotations, sweeping one foot behind her. She wore a sundress or maybe you would call it a spring dress. It was dark gray, a flower pattern, or maybe just swirling dots. It was hard to tell from my hotel room. How I wanted to be that invisible partner.

"I don't even remember putting on my shirt and jeans, and arriving so quickly on the first floor, sitting in the hotel restaurant by the window. I only picked at some eggs on a plate as I looked out at the plaza, the woman still there. I felt myself wanting to be with her. Soon, I was outside walking past elderly women on bicycles who stared at me, somehow sensing that I wasn't Chinese, or maybe that I was very different from anyone they had ever met. As I walked towards the woman that had captivated me, she became obscured by the Tai chi group. The closer I came, the harder she was to see, until I completely lost sight of her. I found myself standing in the middle of the plaza turning in circles trying to find this woman. I wanted nothing more than to slow dance with her. Of course I didn't think it would happen right away, and there was no guarantee that this future was in the cards, but I needed find her and at least introduce myself. I would have asked her if she was studying ballroom. I'm a good conversationalist. And there were many things to talk about—the friendliness of the Chinese, the early retirees making way for the college grads, doing Tai chi in the morning, seemingly health conscious and yet most of the men smoking, but not the women. There were many topics to explore—I could imagine hours going by as we discussed things, comparing, concluding, reevaluating and revisiting. In my mind's eye, there we were like children, whispering stories, giggling and making emphatic gestures. Can you imagine, all this went on in my head?—All these thoughts about someone I had never met—someone I had only seen for a moment.

"Love at first sight—what a ridiculous concept. And yet my mind had completely succumbed to fantasy. Something very strange happened to me. As I was looking for her, I had an almost otherworldly sense that she was the entire feminine collective consciousness in one woman. To be with her would be to find a final resting place for my heart. I don't expect you to understand any of this, but to me, she became the very manifestation of all my dreams. Having seen her and having come so close to encountering her, I experienced something of a mystical state. I believed that my consciousness had been raised by simply being near her. My spirit traveled many places, across oceans, through forests and deserts. I felt dunes of torrid sand become moist soil. I watched seedlings grow and flower. The woman in the gray dress became like the doorway between wakefulness and dreams.

"But where had she gone? She had vanished. I began to wonder if maybe I had imagined her—if it had all been a hallucination. After a few minutes of staring at the Tai chi group I accepted the cruel trick life had tantalized me with. She was nowhere to be found. My original plan had been to see the World Expo, so I decided to take a taxi instead of the hotel shuttle there. When I arrived, the driver argued with me. He thought I was tipping him too much. The Japanese don't tip, so we don't know much about this custom. What I thought was merely being generous, he considered to be a large sum of money. Despite his protest, I left the tip on the seat and went outside.

"Tens of millions would attend the expo that year, mostly Chinese. It was such an ocean of humanity. I met an elderly woman who told me that she had traveled eighteen hours by train to bring her grandson. Many were poor farmers that had never seen a big city, much less something extraordinary and futuristic. I joined the mob moving toward the ticket counter, purchased tickets and then crossed a street and stood in another line outside the main entrance. And then I saw her again, the woman in the gray dress. She was far in front of me, easy to spot because of her dark skin. I anxiously gazed at her, concerned that once she reached the entrance, her splendor would disappear into the throng of people and expo pavilions, which is exactly what happened. Once I had entered the fair, I had to accept that I had lost her again. But after only a few minutes, I saw her. She was standing in front of the South African pavilion, behind her a large mural with the face of Nelson Mandela. She tried to get out of the way of a Chinese person she thought was photographing the mural—she really didn't understand what was going on. So I went to her to offer an explanation. 'It's not the mural they're trying to photograph,' I said in English. 'It's you.'

"'Me?' she asked.

"'They've never seen a westerner before,' I smiled.

"She asked me if I was kidding, almost unable to accept that she was like a celebrity. It must have been her first day in China so she hadn't come to terms with how much of a big deal she was there. Soon, I was rambling on about many things. I told her that I was Japanese. I told her that the cost of the Shanghai Expo was about fifty billion US.—more than the Beijing games. I was afraid that if I stopped talking, she would smile, say goodbye and disappear into the crowd again. But she just listened, and slowly we explored the expo together. Everything seemed to be a reflection of what I saw in her. I was overwhelmed, dazzled by the futuristic pavilions, moved by the colorful lights as the day faded into evening. It was hot and there were so many people there that sometimes one was almost unable to move, and yet I didn't mind. I had been stealing glances of her beautiful face, but had not really turned to study it carefully. When I finally did, I realized that there was more going on than I had understood. I could tell that she knew who I was and also knew many other things that I wasn't ready to know yet. It was as if she could see me from outside time and space. I don't know how I understood all these things just by looking into her eyes, but her expression confirmed everything. And because she returned my stare, I looked away blushing. When I went to look at her again, she had disappeared into the crowd. I didn't even get to ask her what her name was. But as you may have guessed by now, she was Emily Patrick. Some strange manifestation of her, just as the Japanese man she met in the Kyoto subway was a manifestation of me. It seems that we've been at this for a long time, showing ourselves to each other, but not quite being at the right place at the right time in the proper way to make our dreams come true. However, the night that we looked at the stars and slow danced by the pier—that was the night. Everything had become perfect, and we had the rest of our lives to further perfect what was pretty darn perfect. But just as in the story that Emily told, the jealous bitch comes with a weapon to kill and destroy perfect love. You are that evil slut."

"Do you have anything else to say before you die?" Ulysses asked.

"Yes," Toshi said. "My ancestors were samurais. Allow me to take my life honorably with my own sword."

"I can't allow that," Ulysses said. "I'm not going to allow my enemy to arm himself."

"I'm sure you would enjoy watching an evisceration. It would be fascinating for you to see what the sharpest instrument in the world can do to human intestines."

"I would very much like to watch this, but I can't allow it."

"You were very clever in killing Emily in such a way not to leave any ballistics evidence. You shoot me with your gun, and that will no longer be the case. Do you truly not care anymore about your fate? Don't you want to preserve your freedom so that you can fight the globalists or whatever you think you're doing?"

"Let me think about this," Ulysses ruminated. "You'll climb the stairs, reach over to the loft, grab the katana and come back down and sit. I'll distance myself from you. Then you'll pull the sword out of its scabbard, raise it and self-inflict a mortal wound, disemboweling yourself before me. Correct?"

"I can do it exactly as you just stated."

"I very much would like to witness a Japanese ritual suicide."

"A Seppuku," Toshi nodded sadly. "It's usually done with a short blade, but I can do it with one of my katanas. After I'm done, you can decapitate me. It will amaze you how sharp the blade is. It will feel like you're cutting through cake."

"It would be an honor," Ulysses said.

"Do it in such a way that you leave a thin strand connecting the head to the body. The head is not supposed to go flying off."

"Why not?" Ulysses asked. "I think I would enjoy watching your head roll across the room."

"It would not be honorable," Toshi said.

"Fine."

"But just so that you know, there was never any plot by globalists to kill anyone—no plan for robot armies take over the world and serve the elite. There was never any satanic strategy nor were there aliens from other planets intending to do anyone harm. Your life is motivated by fear, and someone exploited this weakness in you deceiving you into believing things that no rational person should consider even for a moment. Yes, governments and corporations are corrupt. Yes, institutions and organization will do what they have to for the sake of self-preservation. Yes, people with too much power have done terrible things to the vulnerable and innocent. But in this case, you're wrong. There do not exist twenty families scheming to commit global genocide-"

"Shut up!" Ulysses shouted. "Of course you would say that. You're one of them. Have you ever heard of Nestor Turk?"

"Not really," Toshi said.

"He is a true patriot. He's read hundreds of books by the world's leading thinkers, and has uncovered the truth behind what is really going on. You're not getting out of this one. Go ahead. Kill yourself. Kill yourself now."

"I'm going to get my katana now."

"Good."

Toshi stood and slowly walked towards the stairs. Ulysses aimed his gun carefully at him.

"You killed the person I love," Toshi said. "Maybe now I will go and be with her."

"Shut up and do it."

"I'll reach over to the loft, slowly take the sword and come back down to sit. Then I'll pull it out of its scabbard and then make a horizontal incision across my abdomen. If you find that you are unable to decapitate me, for whatever reason, tell me and then I'll make a vertical cut and spill everything inside of me. That should do it. Remember, if you use your gun, they'll trace it back to you. So everything should be done by the sword."

"Wait—I've heard of people being able to deflect bullets with swords," Ulysses said with sudden worry.

"I'm not a sword master," Toshi nodded his head. "I'm just a spoiled rich kid that inherited all these ancient relics. The samurai armor you see is about as foreign to me as it is to you. Do you really think that I can deflect a bullet coming at me at almost a thousand miles an hour? Dodging bullets is a proven myth. And actually hitting a projectile at that speed with a sword is absurd. Traveling faster than the speed of sound, the bullet would hit me before I would ever hear the gun fire."

"You're right. Get the sword and disembowel yourself. Then I'll chop your head off. I'll try to leave that strand you want, but I can't promise you anything."

Toshi reached the top of the stairs.

"Don't even think about trying to dive into a room and escaping," Ulysses said. "You're right about not being able to dodge a bullet. I'll get you."

Toshi raised his hands and tried to convey his intention of reaching for the sword and making no sudden moves. He leaned over the stair railing and lifted the katana and scabbard off its stand. Then he slowly descended the stairs with the sword over his head, his hands open, supporting it with his thumbs. Ulysses stepped back about fifteen feet from where Toshi would sit to perform the seppuku ritual. He stood with his legs far apart, holding the gun with both hands, arms extended.

"It's better if I sit on the floor," Toshi said.

"You're already deviating from what we agreed upon," Ulysses said.

Toshi lifted his head and gave Ulysses an earnest look. "We should do this the traditional way. I should be wearing special clothes, but I'm not. I should be served my favorite foods, but that's also not going to happen. At least let me sit on the floor and do this correctly."

"Okay—sit."

Toshi sat on the floor and took off his shirt.

"What are you doing?"

"The sword is too long so I need to grip it by the blade. It's not that I care about cutting my hands, I just don't want to lose my grip."

"Just hurry and get it over with. You've been stalling for a while. There was no need to tell me about your visit to the Shanghai expo or any of that weird stuff about you and Emily."

"What's wrong with stalling?" Toshi said. "Maybe someone will be here to rescue me soon."

"If you don't do this right this second, I'm going to shoot you."

Toshi removed the katana from its scabbard. Then he wrapped his shirt around it and gripped the blade, training it on himself.

"It's funny."

"What's funny?" Toshi snapped.

"When you're about to die, you can see heaven open up before you. You can even see yourself already beyond the gates experiencing it."

"What do you see?" Ulysses asked.

"I see Emily."

# CHAPTER TWENTY FIVE

Salter and Ramos arrived at the home of Toshi Yamamoto several hours later than they had anticipated. An unusual combination of car pile-ups, construction and lane closures had made their trek through Miami Dade County a lengthy tiresome ordeal. The sun was still bright over the water that surrounded the island. They squinted despite the dark sunglasses, lifting their hands to shield themselves from the light refracting off of Toshi's two story villa. Ramos pressed a button to sound the chimes and then knocked on the door.

"I told him we were coming," Salter said. "Where could he be?"

Ramos turned the door knob. "It's open. Should we go in?"

Salter unfastened the snap of his gun holster and held the grip. Ramos did the same. They exchanged nods and entered the house pointing their weapons. What they saw filled them with horror. Never had they seen so much blood. There was a large pool of dark crimson on the white tiles of the living room floor. The walls were splattered with it, as if something—or many things—had been butchered, and then the slaughterhouse had been emptied, leaving behind what was too small to pack and ship. They stood frozen for a long time, unable to form words. Then they searched the house and found that there was no one there.

Eventually the blood was compared to DNA found on Toshi's toothbrush and hairs from his bathtub. It was determined not to be his. When Ulysses' wife reported her husband missing, his DNA was found to be an exact match to the blood, bone fragments and teeth they had found strewn all over the house. Salter and Ramos searched for Toshi for days to question him. They would have been easily convinced that killing Ulysses in his own house was an act of self-defense, but needed a fuller understanding of what happened. Police divers looked for body parts in the waters around the island. The Japanese embassy was notified of Toshi's disappearance. Federico

Carlisomo Jafet, Simeon Suslov and Father Richard Osf were questioned. But all that could be known was that there was a lot of Ulysses' blood, an unfired gun, and no explanation.

Salter met with the family of Emily Patrick and told them that her murderer had most likely been killed while trying to harm someone else. One night, he went home exhausted and perplexed by life. He looked for Emily's video channel, selected a recording and sat back, relaxing and then falling asleep to Emily's soothing voice.

…

In the spring, Toshi met Simeon Suslov for lunch at a restaurant by a road that meandered through a valley in the Swiss Alps. Despite being so close to Italy, they ordered large plates of pasta. Toshi was quiet and Simeon had to make an effort to converse with him.

"You shouldn't have fled," Simeon said, giving up the small talk and striking at the core of the matter.

"I had to," Toshi said.

"Why?"

"It was a shameful thing I did. Besides, anyone could see that I wasn't just killing an intruder. It was a crime of passion. What else would explain such extreme violence? The detectives were supposed to come. They had called and told me they were coming. But they never came. I waited for them until the very end, and only then did I allow myself to do what I did."

"You could hire the best lawyers. Anyone with any skills of persuasion at all could convince a jury that this man had come with a gun to murder you and that you were well with in your right to kill him. So you got a little carried away."

"Simeon," Toshi stopped him. "I had always thought that I would pass through this world without ever bringing harm to another person. But not only did I kill a man. If I'm honest with myself, I have to admit that I took pleasure in what I did. I shredded him to ribbons. I was so angry for what he had done to Emily. And I feel ashamed that I allowed that anger to turn to pleasure, even if it was only for a moment. It's strange how life forces you to make impossible choices. Killing is wrong, but killing a monster seems right. Who am I to think that I'll ever understand what came over me? But one thing is certain, the monster thought he was good, and stood for all good things. Isn't that the way it always is? The opposite extremes actually curve and meet each other to make a circle. The fanatically righteous become the very evil they fear."

Simeon heaved a sigh, bringing his knuckles to his cheek. "Whenever you're ready to return to the world of normalcy, I can help you—just like I helped you hide what was left of-"

"Nothing can ever be normal again. How can I ever forget chopping a man to bits?"

"You can't, but things will get better. Tell me, what was it about Emily that meant so much to you?"

"It's as if I had known her my whole life. I kept seeing glimpses of her—not just glimpses but meeting her over and over. She's always been like a ghost that I see. She's in my thoughts. She's in my dreams."

"Can you see her now?" Simeon asked.

Toshi nodded.

Simeon stuck out his lower lip slightly and returned Toshi's nod. "Can you tell me one of your dreams—I mean can you tell me exactly what you see?"

Toshi looked out at the window at the snowcapped mountains. "What I tell you is more than just a dream."

"It's real. I understand."

"I've had enough girlfriends to understand the common pattern of love. I know that intense physical love doesn't last. I know that in deeper relationships, love is transformed into something more mature and from time to time the physical love is rekindled. I'm not naïve. I know all these things. But what if there's something more? What if you find someone, and through that someone you can see all the way into infinity? What if you meet someone and find that you have an awareness of a greater world—a greater joy?

"Emily…Emily. Yes, it would have been wonderful to hold her longer, to explore the many ways of kissing, to notice pleasure in her eyes, to experience inner peace and delirium all at once, to care only about her happiness as if her delight and satisfaction were saving the world. It would have been wonderful witness her every expression—what I would consider to be the highest form of art, exciting me to the edge of an abyss, my mind ebbing away. It would have been wonderful to rub my lips against her skin, as if I were slipping into a dream brought on by feeling the heat of her neck. I could easily picture her feeling an ever so faint shiver in her body. The fragrance of her perfume, the words spoken with her eyes, her lips becoming rosy with love, all the things about her that expressed mysticism and decadence and dazzling beauty—these things would have pushed me off the precipice.

"All I ever did was slow dance with her, but I could have melted into her. She seemed ethereal to me almost like a Gauguin painting. There's a particular Gauguin painting I'm quite fond of. It's called Spirit of the Dead Watching. A naked Tahitian girl lying on her stomach—such a beautiful painting. The artist said that the title of the painting either refers to the girl imagining a ghost, or a ghost imagining her. I've been thinking a lot about it. I think Emily is like the girl in the painting. You may think she is dead, but to me she is real. And right now, she's imaging me, the ghost."

...

That night, the two ghosts shared a dream. Yes, yes, Emily said with a gorgeous whisper. The yellow Tuscan moon that Toshi had anticipated seeing when arriving in Italy was present, painting the room they were in, glimmering and dancing on Emily's skin. He had no idea where they were nor did he care. They made love in a manner that they understood was outside time, something they would never remember in heaven or earth. He found the softness of her petals to be like the unfolding of the cosmos, billowing and sweet. Her scent was like a glowing ember of incense after being blown out, an offering to atone for everything that had been lost and all the love that had been stolen from them. He could feel her body tense and aching with contentment. The side of her face pushed against a pillow, almost as if looking away in disbelief. Then she closed her eyes tight, as if holding back tears. He felt waves crashing within her. She appeared to him like a deity in the moonlight. He told her that she was beautiful, but she would never know what those words truly meant to him. As he loved her, he found and deciphered even more secrets in her eyes. But she could also see inside of him. In the chambers of his heart, the words echoed. Perfect...Perfect...

###

# ABOUT THE AUTHOR

Carlos Aleman lives in Sunrise, Florida with his wife, Jean.
His website is CarlosAleman.com

www.ingramcontent.com/pod-product-compliance
Ingram Content Group UK Ltd.
Pitfield, Milton Keynes, MK11 3LW, UK
UKHW020142250726
13967UKWH00002B/821